CANDIDE
REDUX

CANDIDE REDUX

HUGH PATRICK

Copyright © 2010 Hugh Patrick

The moral right of the author has been asserted.

Apart from any fair dealing for the purposes of research or private study, or criticism or review, as permitted under the Copyright, Designs and Patents Act 1988, this publication may only be reproduced, stored or transmitted, in any form or by any means, with the prior permission in writing of the publishers, or in the case of reprographic reproduction in accordance with the terms of licences issued by the Copyright Licensing Agency. Enquiries concerning reproduction outside those terms should be sent to the publishers.

Matador
5 Weir Road
Kibworth Beauchamp
Leicester LE8 0LQ, UK
Tel: 0116 279 2299
Email: books@troubador.co.uk
Web: www.troubador.co.uk/matador

ISBN 9781848763197

British Library Cataloguing in Publication Data.
A catalogue record for this book is available from the British Library.

Typeset in 11pt Times by Troubador Publishing Ltd, Leicester, UK

Matador is an imprint of Troubador Publishing Ltd

Printed in Great Britain by the MPG Books Group, Bodmin and King's Lynn

Chapter One

THE MANOR HOUSE

There lived in Sussex, at the country house of Sir Charles Rathbone, a young boy of rare charm and manners. You could read his character in his face. He combined sound judgment with unaffected simplicity. In short, he was Candide. The staff suspected that he was the son of Sir Charles' sister by a poor stranger, whom the young lady could never agree to marry on account of his low position.

Sir Charles was one of the most influential men in the county, and his large manor house had beautiful grounds and a long tree-lined drive. All his employees loved him and worked long hours without complaint. They called him 'Sir' and laughed at his jokes. His wife, whose family and connections made her a person of great importance, entertained with a lavishness which won her still more respect. Her daughter Penelope was a buxom girl of seventeen with a pure complexion; altogether seductive. The son of the house, Penelope's brother, was known as "a chip off the old block."

Candide was in every way worthy of the good Sir Charles' patronage. His schoolmasters gave him good reports and, during the long school holidays, his tutor Pangloss was the recognised authority in the house on all matters of learning. Young Candide listened to his teaching with the unhesitating faith that marked his age and character.

Pangloss taught the doctrine of economic individualism. Every day he proved that the unfettered market provides the best possible allocation of resources. He showed that there can be no charity which does not ultimately cause a greater harm, and that the size of Sir Charles' house and grounds and the virtues of his wife were, without doubt, testament to the wisdom of the market's distribution of resources.

"It is proved," he would say, "that the rich only select from the heap what is precious and most agreeable. They consume little more than the poor and they divide with the poor the produce of all their improvements. They are led by an invisible hand to make nearly the same distribution of the necessities of life which would have been made had the earth been divided into equal portions amongst all its inhabitants."

Candide listened attentively and with implicit belief, for he liked to swim when the weather was warm and he found Penelope extremely beautiful, though he never had the courage to tell her so. Only under such a system, thought Candide, could such beauty be found. Undoubtedly Pangloss was the greatest economist in the whole of England, and consequently, the greatest in all the world.

One day, Penelope was walking near the house in some trees when she saw Dr Pangloss giving a lesson in market forces to her mother's maid, a pretty brunette who seemed eminently teachable. Since Penelope took a great interest in economics, she watched the lecture with breathless fascination. She saw clearly the tutor's invisible hand. Then, in a disturbed and thoughtful state of mind, she returned home filled with a desire for learning. She determined to seek out Candide. On her way to the house she met Candide and blushed. Candide blushed too. Her voice was choked with emotion as she greeted him, and Candide spoke to her without quite knowing what he said.

The following day, as they were leaving the dinner table, Penelope and Candide happened to meet behind a curtain. Penelope dropped her handkerchief and Candide picked it up. She innocently took his hand and he, just as innocently, kissed hers with grace and ardour. Their lips met, their eyes flashed, their knees shook and their hands would not keep still.

Sir Charles, happening to pass the curtain at that moment, observed this interplay of cause and effect. He drove Candide from the house, with vigorous kicks from behind. Penelope fainted and, on coming to, was smacked by Her Ladyship. There was consternation in the most beautiful and richest of mansions.

Chapter Two

TO WORK

Expelled from his earthly paradise, Candide wandered blindly and in tears, casting his eyes towards Heaven, or back towards the finest of houses, where lay the loveliest of daughters. He lay down to sleep at the side of the road; it was snowing heavily.

Next day, numb with cold, he dragged himself to the nearest village, Market Morton. Penniless and faint with hunger and fatigue, he stood gloomily at the door of a pub.

Two men noticed him. "There's a strong looking young fellow," said one to the other, "and he looks as if he could use some cash." They went up to Candide and offered to buy him a drink. "Gentlemen," said Candide, "I am very grateful but I have not the money to pay my share."

"People of your stature can always earn a living," said one of the men. "You know how to lay bricks, don't you?"

"Yes sirs," said Candide, remembering how he had helped the men building a wall around the tennis court.

"Well then, come with us. We'll pay your share and what's more, if you come and work with us you will not go short of money again. After all, that's what men are here for, to help and aid each other."

"You are quite right," said Candide, "for that is what Pangloss used to tell me: that the market will always bring together people to satisfy each others' needs."

So saying, he shook hands with his new employers, who bought him a drink and gave him a contract to sign.

The next day, Candide began work at a building site. He did not find the work particularly easy and the market seemed to give him little reward for his aching limbs and back. But Candide, scrupulously fair, recognised that he was sadly lacking in the training and skills that would allow him to command a better wage. Candide's job was to clean and repair an old outhouse containing some rusty drums holding an unnamed liquid. He was a sensitive youth and it hurt him that his fellow workers gave him and his work such a wide berth.

One fine morning, he took it into his head to leave and walked straight off, thinking it a privilege of men to go wherever they wanted. But he had not gone more than six miles before he was arrested for breach of contract and thrown into a cell. At trial he was offered the fair choice of paying a fine or going to prison. It was useless to declare his belief in individual freedom and say that he wanted neither. So, mindful that he had no money, he elected to go to prison.

Once in prison, he received training in a number of skills, often from his fellow prisoners. Unfortunately, some of his colleagues were less than tolerant of his manners and background and he found himself much beaten and abused.

After two weeks of this poor Candide was pushed back onto the street and cold and hunger once more added to his misery. "I must follow my master's teaching," he said, his teeth chattering. "The individual is always strong if he just puts his mind to it." So saying, he decided to join the army, thinking that at least in this enterprise he would be rewarded with food and a bed.

Chapter Three

OFF TO WAR

The British Army at this time was an upright and honourable institution, a true bastion of freedom and democracy. Unfortunately Candide, in his haste, joined a different army; in some ways even more professional since they fought only where the pay was highest. Candide thought this was odd at first, but he reflected that the market for armed men no doubt contributed to the general good in the same way as any other market and he sailed for Central America with a contented heart.

Scarcely a week had gone by before his troop encountered the enemy. Looking around him as the battle ended, Candide saw that he had become separated from his colleagues. Picking his way over the piles of dead and dying in the village they had just liberated, he contemplated which way to go. His fellow freedom fighters had burned the village to the ground in their eagerness. Old men, crippled with wounds, watched helplessly the death-throes of the butchered women. Among the dying were girls who had been used to satisfy a number of the heroes' natural needs, and had afterwards been disembowelled. Other women, half burnt alive, begged to be put out of their pain. The ground was covered with blood, arms and legs.

As fast as he could, Candide made off to another village. This had recently been liberated by the opposing government forces and its inhabitants had been treated the same way. Treading over quivering limbs and rubble, Candide at length emerged from the war-zone. His thoughts were still full of Mistress Penelope.

For a number of hours Candide wandered lost, looking for his colleagues. On and on he walked, passing through the occasional poor village, but mostly seeing no one. As night fell, he realised that he was once more hungry. He had no money and nothing to sell. "I still have my rifle," thought Candide, "perhaps I can persuade someone to share their food with me."

When he was full, he felt a little better. But he looked down at his torn trousers and shirt and felt the dirt on his hands and in his hair. That night he slept badly by the side of the road and had his rifle stolen. "Oh, how I wish I was back in England," thought Candide.

The next morning he found himself in a village where a man was lecturing a crowd on the virtues of self-discipline. The speaker pointed at him. "Look my friends," he shouted to the crowd, "look at this miserable wretch. He does no work, you can all tell that! He does nothing but lie, sleep, steal and beg. This is why we need to force such people into our glorious work scheme, to teach them responsibility and self-reliance."

"But sir," said Candide, "I agree, for only then will people like me become economically active and live once more in a beautiful house with the beautiful Penelope. It is my fault that I have reached this state, for it certainly cannot be anybody else's!"

"What!" shouted the speaker who, for all his words, did not really welcome competition. "Do you really claim to be a true believer in all the theories of economic liberalism, monetarism, comparative advantage and endogenous neoclassical growth theory?"

"I've never heard of them," admitted Candide, for Pangloss had indeed had his limitations.

"Then you don't deserve to eat! Begone you scrounger. Away wretch! Don't come near me again or you shall suffer for it!"

The speaker's wife had been looking out of the window overhead. Seeing a man who seemed to doubt that a poor country gained by trading with a rich one, she emptied a chamber pot on his head – an example of the excesses to which some are driven by their convictions.

A man passing in the street saw Candide's humiliation, took him home and gave him food and a bath. His benefactor, a kindly merchant named Shara, even offered to give him a job in his poppy harvesting business, for which there was a thriving export market. Candide almost fell at his feet. "My tutor Pangloss was right," he exclaimed, "for he told me that even the most disadvantaged of men can find work if they really look for it!"

Chapter Four

THE IMPORTANCE OF INEQUALITY

Next day, whilst out for a walk, Candide met a beggar covered with sores. The man's eyes were sunk in his head, the end of his nose eaten away, his mouth awry, his teeth black. He spoke in a husky whisper, coughed violently, and seemed to spit out a tooth at every spasm.

Candide was moved more by compassion than revulsion at the sight of this ghastly scarecrow, and gave him the small amount of money Shara had given him. He recoiled in horror, however, when the apparition, gazing at him, burst into tears and fell on his neck.

"Alas," said the poor creature, "don't you recognise your poor Pangloss?"

"What, can it be you, my dear master – and in

so fearful a plight? What disaster has befallen you? Why have you left the finest of houses? What has become of Mistress Penelope, that pearl amongst young ladies, that masterpiece of nature?"

"I am utterly spent," said Pangloss. Candide led him into Shara's stable, where he brought him something to eat. When Pangloss was feeling better, Candide resumed his questions. "And now, please, what of Penelope?"

"She is dead."

At these words Candide fainted, but his friend revived him by shaking him roughly and splashing his face with water. Candide opened his eyes.

"Penelope is dead?" said he. "But how? When? Could no one help or protect her? What did she die of? Was it from grief at seeing her father kick me out of his house?"

"No," said Pangloss, "she was thrown onto the streets when Sir Charles lost his fortune in the stock market crash and killed himself after selling the loveliest of houses to settle all his debts. His wife died of grief and shame and her son, likewise, met an untimely end. Penelope was forced to take up prostitution until she was killed by a violent, drunken client."

Candide fainted again. When he recovered, he cursed the capriciousness of the market, and then asked how and what had brought Pangloss to such a wretched state.

"Alas," said Pangloss, "it was love; love, the comfort of the human race, preserver of the universe, the soul of all feeling creatures; the tender passion of love."

"Ah me," said Candide, "I too have known this love, sovereign of hearts. All it brought me was one kiss and a score of kicks on the backside. But how could so fair a cause produce in you so foul an effect?"

"Well, my dear Candide, you will remember Paquette, that pretty maid of Her Ladyship's? In her arms I tasted love but alas took from her an infection and the disease you see that has so corrupted me."

"I know disease," said Candide, "there is enough of it in this country. But could you not afford treatment?"

"My dear Candide," replied Pangloss, "do you think that after what happened I could afford anything? I was reduced to begging in the street for my food!"

"But how can this be?" asked Candide. "Is this how the market should work: that a man of your intelligence should be reduced to this?"

"Certainly it is," replied the great philosopher. "It is indispensable that disease and illness should constantly threaten complacency and idleness to ensure that people maximise their economic efforts whilst they are healthy and fit. The sick could not be made instantly better without threatening the very principle of inequality which gives the system such dynamism, for where the difference between success and failure is greatest, the maximum effort from both the poor and the rich will be forthcoming. Inequality is the very lifeblood of the marketplace, although we prefer to call it 'incentive', and the general good is best served when individual inequalities are at their most apparent."

"I could listen to you forever," said Candide, "but you must be cured."

"How can I be cured?" said Pangloss. "I haven't got a penny in the world and there's not a doctor anywhere who will see you without a fee."

This last remark decided Candide. He hurried to find Shara and, falling at his feet, painted such a picture of the talents and general usefulness of his old tutor, that the good man did not hesitate to take him in and have him cured at his own expense. Pangloss lost just one eye and the use of a leg. He still had a perfect command of arithmetic and his imagination was unimpaired. Shara appointed him as his accountant and for the next two months, Pangloss earned enough through his mastery of tax minimisation to keep both himself and Candide. Candide began to settle down in his new home, though his heart was still heavy at the loss of his beloved Penelope.

One day, Shara announced that they must go to Caracas on business and he set out across the mountains, taking his two philosophers with him. On the journey, Pangloss explained that the workings of the market ensured that if all individuals followed their own interests, then the invisible hand would lead them towards actions which benefited the general good. Shara smiled ruefully. "In this backward country," he said, "we are not so civilised as others. No, we are altogether closer to nature, where each must fight for himself and needs no excuse or justification for his victory over the weak and less fortunate."

"The same invisible hand!" exclaimed the one-eyed doctor. "It does not have to be a conscious decision; the general good is still always improved simply by each person doing what is best for themselves."

While he was listening to this argument, Candide noticed that the roads had become full of people, rushing in all directions and shouting. In seconds they were enveloped in the swell of a terrible riot.

Chapter Five

THE DEATH OF SHARA

The car slowed to a halt as the crowd pressed around it. The driver, one of Shara's servants, pulled the car to the left and for a moment they escaped into a side-street and relative safety.

"Quick! Out of the car!" shouted Shara. "The desperados!"

Candide was too shocked to speak, but he stumbled out of the car into the filthy road and looked about him. A mass of the poorest people he had ever seen ran wild before his eyes. Their poverty hung over them like a cloud, proclaiming itself in every face and limb. He turned to see his old tutor and his benefactor standing in the shelter of the car, trembling. The worthy Shara was busy ripping the gold from his neck and fingers and stuffing the jewels into his pockets, taking care to rip and muddy his shirt as he did so.

"Who are they?" cried Candide above the noise of the riot.

"It is the poor of the city," replied Shara, "there has long been a famine among the lower classes and they claim to be starving."

"But the coffee fields thrive everywhere," Candide would have said if he had had time to think, "these people must be very inefficient for their harvests to fail in such a fertile land."

The crowd looked as if it would pass them by in its search for better pickings, and the last of the rioters had almost passed when Shara's expensive shoes and extravagant figure caught attention. Before Candide could lift a finger to help, the mob had seized his benefactor and carried him away, despite his weight. His abductors soon tired of carrying him and they dashed him into the dust and trampled him underfoot. Candide rushed across the road and was in time to catch a glimpse of a tortured face before the figure was once more swallowed up by the crowd.

"Oh Shara!" cried Candide, "my friend Shara!"

He wanted to throw himself into the crowd after him but his tutor, Pangloss, stopped him by explaining that these deaths were no doubt part of a painful but necessary adjustment to the famine from which this country suffered. Candide was initially too grief-stricken to join with his tutor's satisfaction of the workings of the market, even in such circumstances. The economist was about to take his pupil back to first principles when the army arrived and took action to quell the riot, decreasing the future demand for food considerably. Candide and Pangloss were too scared to run away and they were arrested and taken to a police station. A number of men spent some time demanding of Candide what he knew, but Candide had had a confusing morning and was an altogether unsatisfactory prisoner.

Chapter Six

ON TRIAL

When he regained consciousness, Candide found that he could not move. The soles of his feet had been burnt, his back had been lashed raw, and his toe and finger nails had long since been removed.

"For heaven's sake," he said to Pangloss, "fetch me some water, I'm dying!"

"This treatment is not necessarily bad," replied Pangloss. "It is often necessary to protect the majority from a minority who, in their ignorance, do not appreciate the benefits of the prevailing system. Thus the use of a little force, with careful application, can be a necessary adjunct to a free economy and ultimately aid even those against whom it is used."

"Nothing is more likely," said Candide, "but some water, for pity's sake!"

"Likely?" exclaimed the philosopher, "I maintain that it is proved. In Chile...."

Pangloss broke off as he noticed that Candide had fainted and he brought him a little water from a bowl which stood in the corner.

The following day, Candide regained enough strength to be put on trial, Pangloss by his side. Pangloss tried to explain to the court that, far from being rioters, they were actually enthusiastic supporters of the regime.

But the government had decided that the sight of some executions would help concentrate the peasants' minds. The two friends were found guilty on all charges and were sentenced to be shot by firing squad. Candide was overcome.

"Oh sirs," he said, "I beg you for mercy. We are strangers to your country and meant no harm. We are not evil communists; on the contrary, we embrace the ways of free men."

The judges were impressed by Candide's argument and commuted the sentences to hanging. On the appointed day, a crowd gathered to cheer the hanging of Pangloss while Candide was flogged in time to the national anthem. To his surprise however, he was then not hanged but thrown into the street, where another riot seemed to have started.

The terrified Candide stood covered in blood and trembling with fear and confusion.

"Had it just been a matter of being flogged," he thought, "why then I might have stood it. Indeed, I would have been happy enough just to have not been hanged! But when it comes to dear Pangloss, the greatest of economists, why did he have to die? And Shara, and all the other casualties of the riot? And Lady Penelope, that pearl amongst young women, why did she have to meet such an end?"

As he was tottering feebly away from the place where he had been tortured and flogged, an old woman came up to him and said: "Be of good cheer, child, and follow me."

Chapter Seven

PENELOPE RE-FOUND

Candide was not at all of good cheer, but he followed the old woman nonetheless. She led him to a run-down house, where she gave him some soothing ointments, food and drink, and showed him to a clean little bed, beside which hung a suit of clothes. "Eat, drink and sleep," she said "and may the Lord and all his saints watch over you. I shall be back tomorrow."

Candide, who was still dazed by all that he had seen and suffered, and still more so by the old woman's kindness, sought to kiss her hand. "It is not *my* hand you should kiss," she said. "I shall be back tomorrow. Rub the ointments into your wounds, eat and sleep."

Despite all his sorrows, Candide ate and slept. Next morning, the old woman brought him breakfast, examined his wounds and applied the ointments herself. Later, she brought him lunch and supper. The day after, she again brought him lunch. Candide kept on questioning her: who was she, what was the reason for all her kindness, how could he show his gratitude? But she did not answer.

On the evening of the second day, the old woman came again to Candide's room, but this time brought no supper.

"Come with me," she said, "and do not speak a word."

Taking him by the arm, she led him about a quarter of a mile into the country, to a lonely house surrounded by gardens and fields.

A small door was answered to her knock, and she led Candide by some back stairs to a richly decorated bedroom. The old woman led him to an elegant couch and then left him, shutting the door. Candide felt that the last few weeks had seemed like a nightmare, and that the present was also a dream, but a pleasant one.

Shortly, the old woman came back, supporting a trembling young lady of majestic build, richly bejewelled and wearing a veil.

"Take off her veil," the old woman said, and Candide shyly did so. To his amazement, it was – yes, indeed, it was! – Mistress Penelope! He fell, speechless, at her feet, whilst she fell backwards upon the sofa. The old woman gave them both a drink and they recovered enough composure to speak. At first they could utter only broken phrases, interrupting each other's questions and answers; gasping, weeping and exclaiming. The old woman advised them to make less noise, and left them alone.

"So is it really you," said Candide, "alive and here in South America? You were not forced on to the streets, to sell yourself to strangers and be beaten?"

"Indeed that happened," said Penelope, "but such accidents are not always fatal."

"But did your father and mother and brother all die?"

"Alas, it is too true!" She wept.

"And how have you come to be here? How did you know that I was here? And by what strange adventure did you contrive to have me brought to this house?"

"I will tell you the whole story. But first you must tell me what has befallen you, ever since that day when you gave me that innocent little kiss and my father kicked you out of the manor house."

Candide obeyed devotedly. He was still in a state of bewilderment, and also somewhat distraught by the pain from his wounds, so that he spoke in a quavering whisper. He gave her a straightforward account of all that had happened to him since their separation. Penelope kept turning up her eyes in horror. She wept to hear of the death of Shara. Then she told her own story, whilst Candide avidly listened and gazed upon her.

Chapter Eight

PENELOPE'S STORY

"One morning, I awoke to hear my mother screaming. I rushed downstairs to see her bent over the figure of my father, already drawing his last breaths. He had lost his entire fortune in the stock market crash. After that morning, our prospects rapidly worsened until it seemed that everything was against us. Sir Charles left us with many debts and we were forced to sell the most beautiful of manor houses. My mother was unable to adjust to our new situation and died a pauper's death. My brother died soon afterwards, an alcoholic with a gambling addiction. I had neither skills nor qualifications, despite all Pangloss' teaching, and I was forced to forget my breeding and become a common whore. How I hated those men who used me so! Still, we must all earn a living somehow, I suppose.

"Eventually one client insisted on something too terrible. No, my dear Candide, I cannot possibly tell you. I resisted, struggling and biting and the beast gave me a wound on my left thigh – I still bear the scar."

"Do let me see it!" said Candide ingenuously.

"You shall, but let me proceed."

"Please do."

"A policeman heard my screams, battered down the door and came into the room. He noticed I was bleeding and felt sorry for me. He drew his truncheon and hit the man on the head. Unfortunately, the policeman was too enthusiastic and the man died as he fell. Seeing that I was homeless and, in any event, had been witness to the killing, the policeman decided, in his kindness, to take me into his house. I used to wash his shirts for him and cook his meals. But there is no denying that he found me pretty as well as useful and I soon discovered that there were other duties for me to perform. He was quite handsome in a way, but apart from that I can say little for him. He had not much intelligence and no understanding of economics. Clearly he had not been taught by the worthy Pangloss, God bless his soul.

"At the end of three months, he arranged for me to go to live with a South American businessman whom I understood he had crossed and wished to make amends. I was very grateful to the policeman for saving me from a life of prostitution, and for looking after me so selflessly, so I went willingly and have fared even better under my new patron."

She looked around at the splendour of the bedroom in which they sat.

"I used to think that there was no place as beautiful as our old house, but now I see that I was wrong.

"Anyway, one day a general in the army noticed me in the street and leered at me quite disgracefully. He sent a message to my businessman to say that he had something to discuss with me in private. Everyone here pays the army the utmost respect and so I was taken very promptly to the general's house in the centre of the city.

"When he heard of my birth and breeding he told me that I was degrading myself by living with a common merchant and offered to look after me himself. The generosity of my businessman, however, knew no bounds and he refused to give up his charge, so the general sent some soldiers to help persuade him. Even then he would only agree to share the burden of keeping me.

"Thus the upkeep of this house is paid for by both of them jointly and they have the duty of looking after me on alternate days. On Mondays, Wednesdays and Fridays I am the charge of the businessman, and the general's on the other days of the week. Sunday is a day of rest, for they are both religious men. This agreement has now lasted for some months, but not without disputes, for they often fail to agree whether one day ends at midnight or at the following morning. However, on the whole they are both happy.

"In the course of time, the general invited me to join him at a public execution. I had an excellent seat and, in the interval between Mass and the executions, refreshments were served.

"I was dreadfully shocked as the executions started but imagine my amazement and horror when I saw a figure resembling Pangloss! I rubbed my eyes, gazed at him closely, and saw him hanged. I swooned.

"Scarce had I recovered my senses, when I beheld you, awaiting the same fate. That was the height of my horror, consternation, grief and despair. I will confess that your skin was even smoother and more lustrous than the policeman's! I asked the general who you were. He laughed and said 'Just another rabble-rouser', but seeing my anxious face and my pleas on your behalf, he decided to demonstrate his authority by having your sentence commuted to flogging.

"As I watched you being flogged, I was almost beside myself with frenzy, asking myself how the wise Pangloss and the good Candide could have come to such an end. My mind went back to my father's suicide and my mother's death, to the insolence of the man who wounded me, and to my life as housekeeper and courtesan to a policeman, a businessman and a general. But above all, my mind dwelt on the kiss you gave me behind the curtain that day when I saw you for the last time.

"I thanked God for bringing you back to me after so many trials, and ordered my old servant to take care of you and to bring you here as soon as she could. She has carried out my orders well and I have the inexpressible delight of seeing you again.

"But you must be ravenous with hunger, and I, too, have a great appetite. Let us first have supper."

They sat down at the table and after supper returned to the magnificent sofa. They were still there when the businessman entered. It was Wednesday, and he had come to exercise his rights and enjoy what he had paid for, and to unfold the tenderness of his love.

Chapter Nine

DEATHS OF THE BUSINESSMAN AND THE GENERAL

The businessman was of an excitable and jealous nature. "So, you English bitch!" he said. "Is not the general enough for you, that I must share you with this rascal?" He pulled a knife from his pocket and rushed at Candide, thinking him unarmed. But the stalwart Candide had received, along with the suit of clothes the old woman had given him, a weapon of his own. Despite his naturally gentle and peaceable nature, he laid the businessman stone dead at Penelope's feet.

"My God!" she cried. "What will become of us? A man killed in my bedroom! If the police come, we are undone!"

"If Pangloss had not been hanged," Candide replied, "that great philosopher would have given us good advice on this emergency. Since we have not him, let us consult the old woman."

She was a shrewd old lady, and very willing to give advice. As she was doing so, the door opened again. It was an hour after midnight and therefore the beginning of Thursday, a day which belonged to the general. He was now confronted with Candide, that recently flogged villain, standing with dagger drawn, a corpse on the floor, Penelope cowering with fright and the old woman giving her advice.

A train of thought now passed clearly and rapidly through Candide's mind: "If this soldier calls for assistance, he will certainly have me shot, and perhaps Penelope too. He has had me cruelly flogged. He is my rival. I have got into the way of killing people. There is no time to hesitate." Before the general could recover from his surprise, Candide stabbed him through the heart and laid him beside the businessman.

"And now there's another of them!" wailed Penelope. "This is unpardonable. We are done for. Our last hour has come! But how could you – you, who has such a mild temper – bring yourself to kill a businessman and a general, all in two minutes?"

"Beautiful Penelope," said Candide, "when a man is in love, is jealous, and has been flogged, he does the most surprising things."

"There is a small car in the garage," said the old woman, "let Candide go and start it and drive it to the front of the house. Madam, you must collect all the gold and diamonds you have earned, for we will need money. Come, let us make haste!"

Candide ran downstairs and found the car. Penelope and the old woman joined him at the front door, and they drove for hours without stopping. Meanwhile the police had entered the house. The general was buried with full military honours, the businessman thrown into an unmarked grave.

By this time, Candide, Penelope and the old woman were already at an inn in the little town of Aracena, where they were engaged in an earnest discussion.

Chapter Ten

VOYAGE TO THE INTERIOR

Penelope wept. "How can we have sold that precious jewellery for so little?" she said. "What shall we live on? What are we to do?" All her gold and diamonds had been sold for no more than a few pesetas. "Where can I find another businessman or general to give me some more?" she sobbed.

"But Penelope," said Candide, "remember that Pangloss often used to demonstrate that there is no such thing as intrinsic value and nothing is worth more than someone is prepared to pay for it. Unfortunately that man was the only bidder. Have you nothing left at all, dearest Penelope?"

"Not a penny."

"Then what is our course of action?"

"I could sell myself," said Penelope.

"You must sell the car," said the old woman. "We can catch a bus to the port on the river tomorrow, and we have no need of it after that."

A travelling salesman, who was sitting nearby, bought the car for another handful of coins and the next day they arrived at the port. The town was full of soldiers preparing for an expedition against insurgents in the interior, up river. Profiting from his service with the army, Candide was able to demonstrate his proficiency in small-arms drill, ambushing and counter-insurgency measures. He displayed such speed, initiative, morale and efficiency that he was given command of a company. Thus, as a captain, he was able to take on board with him Penelope and the old woman.

During the voyage, they spent much time discussing poor Pangloss' doctrines. "I am sure," said Candide, "that only a completely free market will ensure the optimal distribution of resources and the greatest happiness for all, but the poverty of individuals is so evident and the general good sometimes so intangible that it is difficult at times to see clearly."

"I love you with all my heart," said Penelope, "but for my part I have little faith in a system that allows the great Pangloss and your good self to be brought to such ruin."

"But Penelope, it is the capriciousness of the

market that is its very essence. Who would work so hard if they felt secure?"

"I hope you are right. But I wish I had not had to learn that lesson so often and so harshly."

"You moan and complain," said the old woman, "but you have not suffered half of what I have."

Penelope could hardly help laughing at this seemingly ridiculous assertion. "My good woman," she said, "unless you have lost twice the riches that I once had, and slept with twice the number of men; unless you have lost two fathers and two mothers and beheld four rich benefactors killed before your eyes – I do not see how you can claim to have endured twice as much misery as I have. Add to this that I was born the daughter of a knight, one of the richest men in England, yet have since been a whore and a kitchen maid."

"Mistress, I have never told you my origin. And if I were to tell you of my life, you would not speak so hastily."

Candide and Penelope were eager to know what the old woman meant. She told them her story.

Chapter Eleven

THE OLD WOMAN'S STORY – I

"My eyes were not always bloodshot and red-rimmed; my nose did not always touch my chin, nor was I always a servant.

"I am the daughter of the colonial ruler of Zampatu, once a wealthy country in Africa. Until the age of sixteen, I was brought up in a mansion to which none of your houses of England would serve as stables. A single one of my dresses was worth more than all your fortune.

"I grew in beauty, grace and talent, in the midst of pleasures, homage and fair expectations. Already I inspired men with love. Already my bosom was forming – and what a bosom! White, firm and shaped like a statue of Venus. My eyebrows were black, my eyes flashed brighter than the stars – or so the poets told me. The maids who dressed and undressed me fell into ecstasies when they beheld me before and behind, and all the men would willingly have changed places with them.

"I was engaged to the eldest son of the leading family amongst the settlers. What a man! As handsome as myself, crammed full of sweetness and charm, brilliantly witty and aflame with love. I loved him as one loves for the first time: with obsessive fervour.

"The nuptials were to be of unprecedented splendour, with festivities and a grand ball. Songs and poems were written in my praise – all of them execrable. The moment of my supreme happiness was at hand when my betrothed, persuaded by his friends to enjoy one last night of merriment, drank too much and fell into a coma. He died less than two hours later of blood poisoning.

"But that was a mere trifle. My mother, who was in despair at the turn of events, although her affliction was less than mine, resolved to remove herself and me from the scene of the tragedy. We enjoyed use of a fine estate in the bush, for which we now set out. During our journey we were attacked by rebels. Our bodyguards fought like bodyguards do: that is, when they saw which way the battle was going, they flung themselves to their knees, laid down their arms and begged for mercy.

"They were forthwith stripped naked, as were my mother, our maids and myself. It is amazing how expert these men were at undressing people. But what astonished me more is that they thrust their fingers into a region where women, as a rule, only allow another part to enter. At first I thought this very strange – it is remarkable how travel broadens the mind – but I learnt later that the purpose was to discover if we had concealed any diamonds. The practice has been established from time immemorial among the highly efficient rebel forces and their colonial opponents. I am told that many groups never neglect it when they make a capture of either sex.

"I need not tell you how hard it is for a young woman of such breeding to be led off into the jungle as a prisoner. You can likewise imagine what we had to suffer during the journey. My mother was still very handsome, and our maids had more charms than were to be found in all the rest of Africa. As for myself, I was enchanting; I was grace and beauty itself – and I was a virgin. I did not remain one long; the prize that had been reserved for my fiancé was snatched from me by the captain of the rebel band, a hideous brute of a man, who positively thought he was doing me an honour.

"Indeed, both my mother and I must have had

very strong constitutions to withstand all that we endured until our arrival in the neighbouring country, where the rebels had their base. But I shall not waste time on further relating such commonplace matters.

"At the time of our arrival, the country was awash with blood. The majority tribe, the Xendi, comprising fifty-five percent of the population, had attacked the minority tribe, the Rantu, who comprised forty-five percent of the population, falling to thirty percent in recent months. Of course, attack is the most equitable form of defence and the Rantu did not hesitate to take their own measures, increasing their proportion of the population back to forty-five percent of a much reduced total. The whole country was a field of continuous slaughter.

"As soon as we arrived at the main base, a rival group, hostile to our captain, came to take away his booty. Next to his dollars and diamonds, we were the most valuable things he had. A battle ensued, such as you would never see in England. They fought with the fury of tigers and lions to see who should have us. One man seized my mother by the right arm, my captain's lieutenant seized her by the left leg, another man took her left arm, and another, her right leg. Almost all the women were thus torn apart between four men.

"My captain kept me hidden and with drawn

pistol, tried to shoot any who stood in his way. Ultimately my mother and all our maids were torn to pieces by the monsters who fought for them. Captives and captors, rebels and rivals, and lastly my captain himself, were all slain, and I was left half dead upon a heap of carcasses.

"Similar scenes were being enacted across the country but nothing was ever done to intervene in the affairs of a sovereign state.

"I disengaged myself with difficulty from the pile of bloody corpses, and dragged myself beneath a large lemon tree on the bank of a nearby stream. Here, I collapsed from fright, weariness, horror, despair and hunger, and my crushed body yielded to an oblivion which was nearer fainting than to sleep.

"In this state of weakness and insensibility, between life and death, I felt myself pressed upon by something that moved up and down on my body. Opening my eyes, I saw a man of good appearance who was sighing and muttering: "Oh, what a disaster to be impotent at this time!"

Chapter Twelve

THE OLD WOMAN'S STORY – II

"Astonished to hear these words, I told him that there were worse misfortunes in the world than what he complained of. I briefly described to him the horrors that I had passed through, and fell back into a swoon.

"The man carried me to a house, where he had me put to bed and given food. He waited on me, comforted and flattered me, vowing that he had never seen anything so beautiful as myself, and never before regretted so much the loss of his powers.

"A long time ago I was short of money," he said "and I agreed to take part in a trial for a new drug, but the side-effects were serious and I have been impotent ever since. But, wait, are you not the daughter of the esteemed ruler of Zampatu? I knew you when you were six years old. Already at that age you promised to be as beautiful as you have become."

"Yes, I am." I replied. "My mother lies only four hundred yards away, torn in four pieces, beneath a heap of dead…."

"We exchanged accounts of our adventures. He worked for the embassy and had been sent to negotiate a diplomatic treaty with the Xendi (or the Rantu) to secure an agreement to sell arms and aircraft to the government.

"My mission has been accomplished," said the impotent man. "I am planning to return to Zampatu and will escort you back there. What a disaster, however, to be impotent!"

"I thanked him with tears of joy. Thereupon, instead of conducting me home, he carried me to the capital city and sold me to a mining executive.

"Soon afterwards an epidemic broke out, the result of poor sanitation and nutrition amongst the locals. Have you ever seen a proper plague, mistress?"

"No," said Penelope.

"If you had, you would confess that a riot or a rebellion were as nothing – and it was very common in Africa."

"I was one of those who fell ill. Picture to yourself the plight of a girl of great breeding and sensibility, who, within three months, had suffered want and slavery, had been ravished almost daily, had seen her mother torn into four pieces, had passed through famine and war, and was now dying of disease far from home!

"In the end, I did not die. But the miner and many others, rich and poor, were swept away.

"When the epidemic had spent its first fury, a sale was held of the miner's possessions and I moved in with a trader in import/export. I then moved to another trader based in Dar Es Salaam, then to Cairo and then to Istanbul, where I fell in with drug dealers and became addicted. I was forced to sell a kidney to make ends meet and ended up as a kitchen maid at an inn. I grew old in poverty and degradation, remembering always where I had come from. A hundred times I wished to kill myself, but my love of life persisted. As miserable as was my position then, yet I clung to the hope that I would rise up once again. This ridiculous weakness is perhaps one of the most fatal of our faults. For what could be more stupid than to go on hoping that life will suddenly change for the better, when all the evidence points the other way?

"In the countries through which my destiny has led me, I saw a prodigious number of men and women who worked every hour of every day and yet barely had enough to eat. Living each day as servants in all but name as others profited from their labours.

"My last employ was with the businessman who brought me here and set me to attend to you, my fair lady. I have attached myself to your fortunes, and have been more concerned with your adventures than with my own. I should not have even spoken to you of my mishaps, had you not provoked me a little into telling my story.

"In short, mistress, I know much of the world. Ask all of the men on this boat to tell you their tale and if there is a single one of them who has not many times cursed his fortune, and sworn that he was the most wretched of men, I give you leave to throw me into the river."

Chapter Thirteen

THE GOVERNOR OF FREETOWN

After hearing the old woman's story, Penelope paid her the respect due to a person of her rank and merit. On her suggestion, she asked the other men, one after another, to relate their life stories, and she and Candide had to admit that the old woman was right.

"It is a pity," said Candide, "that wise Pangloss was hanged, since he could have discoursed to us admirably on the general benefit that must flow from such individual misery, and I should have been bold enough to offer some respectful objections."

On reaching their destination, the river port of Freetown, Penelope, Candide and the old woman paid a visit to the Governor. He was called Don Fernando d'Ibarro y Figueora y Mascarenes and his behaviour befitted a man with so many names. In conversation with men, his air of noble disdain, uptilted nose, affected accent and stilted manner made everyone long to hit him. For women, he had an insatiable passion.

Penelope seemed, to the Governor, the most beautiful thing he had ever seen. He enquired whether she was Candide's wife. His manner alarmed Candide, who dared not say that she was his wife, since she was not, nor that she was his sister, since she was not that either. Although such a useful lie of this sort would have had many historical precedents, Candide was too honest for such deceit.

"Mistress Penelope," he said, "intends to do me the honour of marrying me, and we beg your Excellency to grace the impending ceremony with your presence."

Don Fernando d'Ibarro y Figueora y Mascarenes twirled his moustache, smiled sourly and ordered Candide to go and inspect his troop. Left alone with Penelope, he declared his passion, and swore that he would marry her himself the next day, in church or otherwise: her beauty was such that it was all one to him. Penelope asked for a quarter of an hour's reflection. She wanted the advice of the old woman.

"Mistress," said the old woman, "you are a

lady by birth and upbringing, but you have not a penny to your name. If you choose, you could be the wife of the governor of all this country, who has a very fine moustache too. Is it for you to pride yourself on fidelity? It is a luxury very few can afford. You have lived and worked on the streets. A businessman and a general have both enjoyed your favours. These misfortunes perhaps carry their own privileges. If I were you, I should have no hesitation in marrying the governor, and making Candide's fortune."

That same day, another boat arrived in Freetown, carrying detectives and armed police. The flight of Penelope and Candide was by now known. The man who had bought Penelope's gold and jewels had been caught trying to re-sell them for a large profit. He had escaped prosecution by giving full descriptions of the fugitives and their direction of travel. The car and their flight up river had also been traced. The police had now landed and already the rumour spread that they had come for the murderers of the esteemed general.

The clever old woman realised the situation at once. "You cannot run away," she said to Penelope, "and you have nothing to fear. It was not you who killed the general. Besides, the governor here is in love with you, and he will not suffer you to be ill-treated. Stand your ground."

Then she hurried to Candide. "Flee," she said, "or you will be captured and shot within the hour."

He had not a moment to lose. But how could he bring himself to part from Penelope, and where was he to go?

Chapter Fourteen

FLIGHT TO PARAGUAY

Candide had brought with him to Freetown a young valet of the sort that once commonly served the officers of any respected army. He was one quarter native, having been born in Honduras of a Japanese father. He had been, at various times, a choirboy, a sailor, a student, a drug-runner, a soldier and a beggar. His name was Cacambo, and he had a great affection for Candide – which indeed the latter well deserved.

Cacambo quickly secured a serviceable jeep. "Come, master," he said, "let us take the old woman's advice and be off without more ado."

"My dearest Penelope," said Candide, weeping, "must I leave you at the very moment the Governor was going to preside at our wedding? What will become of you so far from home?"

"She must do as well as she can," said Cacambo. "Some people can always look after themselves. God provides for them. Let us be off."

"But where can we go? What shall we do without Penelope?"

"Holy mercy! You were on your way to fight the socialist insurgents; let us fight on their side. I know the roads, and can lead you to their country. They will be delighted to have a captain who knows the government drill and tactics. You will make a fortune, if we play it well. When you don't get what you want from one side, it is often the way that you can get it from the other. It is always a delight to see and do new things."

"Then you have been in Paraguay before?"

"Indeed I have; I was studying in the university in the capital city when the revolution first broke out. I know its streets backwards. And what an admirable country it is! The old landlords have all been banished and their estates placed in collective ownership. The peasants still do not own any land themselves, but take comfort from the fact that the socialists now rule in their name. They make war against the neighbouring countries, financed by oil revenues from the concessions granted by the previous regime. It is a masterpiece of rational and just rule!

"But let us make haste; you have rare good

fortune in store for you. How pleased they will be to learn that they are getting a captain of the government army!"

Before long they came to the frontier post. Cacambo told the guard that a very important man wished to talk to his commanding officer. The main guard was turned out and Candide and Cacambo were disarmed and their jeep driven away. The sergeant of the guard told them that they must wait as the commanding officer needed authorisation in order to speak to them, and in any event, it was siesta.

"But the captain and I are perishing with hunger," said Cacambo, "and the captain is an Englishman who does not take siesta. Could we not at least eat while we wait for him?"

The sergeant immediately reported what he had been told to the commandant. "If he is English, I must speak to him," said the latter, "bring him to my office."

Candide was conducted to the largest of the buildings beside the frontier post. The interior was well decorated and air-cooled. An excellent breakfast waited on the sideboard. Whilst his troops ate maize from wooden baskets outside in the hot sun, the commandant entered the room.

He was a handsome man, round-faced, fair and freshly coloured, with finely arched eyebrows, bright eyes and red lips. He carried himself boldly with a bearing that was more European. On his orders, Candide and Cacambo were given back their arms.

Candide shook hands with the commandant and they sat down at the table.

"So you are English?", said the commandant, in that language.

"Yes sir." The two men suddenly looked at each other with amazement and emotion.

"From what part of England do you come?"

"From Sussex. I was born in a country house near Market Morton."

"Oh, heavens, can it be true?"

"What a miracle!"

"Can it be you?"

"It is not possible!" They both reeled backwards, and then embraced, weeping.

"So you, the commanding officer of this frontier post in Paraguay, are the fair Penelope's brother! But I thought you dead! How come you, Sir Charles' son, to be a socialist army officer? What a strange world! Ah, Pangloss, how would you have explained this, if you had not been hanged!"

The attendant soldiers, who had been about to serve breakfast, withdrew on the commandant's order. With continued exclamations of amazement and goodwill, they again clasped each other in their arms, their faces wet with tears.

"You will be still more overcome," said Candide, "when I tell you that Mistress Penelope, your sister, is not dead, as you supposed, but is in perfect health."

"Where is she?"

"Not far from here, at the house of the Governor of Freetown. I came here to fight you."

Throughout a long conversation, they continued to marvel more and more, talking volubly and hanging on each other's words, with shining eyes. They lingered long at the table, waiting for the provincial commander to join them. Meanwhile the commandant told his story.

Chapter Fifteen

THE KNIGHT'S SON

"I shall never forget the dreadful day when I saw my father dead and my mother's heart broken. My fortune was ruined and I was thrown onto the charity of the state, but it was not easy after a lifetime of luxury. I had hardly realised, as I listened to Pangloss' teachings all those years ago, that they would be one day so directly relevant to me. But our tutor was right. I determined to become rich once more and build a fortune to rival that of my father's. I tried the world of business but had no capital myself and it proved impossible to trace my father's partners and acquaintances. Eventually, I became a journalist and was sent here to cover the insurgency. I had not been here three months when I volunteered to join them and became an officer as you see. I still send my reports to my newspaper in London and my career seems in excellent shape.

"But is it really true that my sister Penelope is with the Governor of Freetown?" Candide solemnly assured him that it was so, and again tears trickled down their cheeks. The commandant repeatedly embraced Candide, calling him his 'brother' and 'saviour'.

"Perhaps, dear Candide," he said, "we shall enter the city together as victors and recover my sister."

"That is all I desire, for I intend to marry her, and still hope to do so."

"What, insolent fellow! You would have the impudence to seek to marry my sister, the daughter of a knight of the realm? Really, you have some cheek to even speak to me of such a plan!"

Candide was thunderstruck. "My good sir," he said, "what is all the breeding in the world? I have rescued her from the clutches of a businessman and a general. She is grateful to me and wishes to marry me. Master Pangloss always told me that all men have equal potential. I shall marry her, depend on it!"

"We shall see about that, villain!" said the brother, and struck Candide across the face with his pistol. Candide caught hold of his wrist and a shot was fired, straight into the commandant's heart. Candide burst into tears.

"Oh God!" he said, "I have killed my old friend, my brother-in-law. I am the mildest man in the world, yet I have already killed three men!"

Cacambo, who was standing guard at the door, came to see what had happened. "Nothing remains but to sell our lives dear," said his master. "Someone will undoubtedly have heard the gun. We must prepare to die bravely." But Cacambo had been in many such scrapes before, and kept calm. In a few seconds he had stripped the commandant of his uniform and put it on Candide, gave him the officer's peaked cap and pulled it down over his eyes.

"Quick, to the jeep!" he said. "Everybody will take you for an officer on a tour of inspection. We shall have passed back over the frontier before they even start to look for us."

With these words he rushed ahead, crying in Spanish: "Make way, make way for the commandant!"

Chapter Sixteen

THE NATIVES AND THE WILD PIG

By the time the officer's death was known in the camp, Candide and his valet were beyond the frontier post. Cacambo had providently filled his backpack with bread, ham, fruit and water.

They drove on into an unexplored and wild region, until they came to a beautiful meadow, cut across by streams. Here they stopped and got out of the car. Cacambo suggested that they eat, and started to do so. "How can you ask me to eat ham," said Candide, "when I have killed Sir Charles' son, and am doomed never to see Penelope again? What is the use of dragging out a wretched existence, far from her, in remorse and despair?" Nevertheless, he ate.

The sun was now setting. The wanderers

heard some faint cries in the forest. They rose hastily to their feet, with the disquiet that is caused by any unexpected event in an unknown country.

The cries they now perceived came from a group of men, clearly natives of the jungle, rushing into the clearing in pursuit of a wild pig. As Candide watched, the wretched animal tried to break back into cover and was brought to ground in front of him by a thrown spear. The natives cried with joy and surrounded the writhing body, hacking at it with knives until the squeals stopped and the carcass lay still, covered in blood. Candide was not used to such barbarism. He leapt out into the clearing and demanded to know why such savagery was necessary. The natives were unimpressed and took both travellers prisoner.

They were led into a poor village of mud huts deep in the jungle. "We shall certainly be either boiled or roasted alive," said Candide, who had read widely when he was young. "How Pangloss would have liked to study such a primitive society! The individual acts so as to enhance the greater good, said he. That may be, but I take little consolation from losing Mistress Penelope and then being impaled on a spit by a tribe of natives."

"Do not lose hope," said Cacambo, "I understand a little of these people's language. I will seek to buy our freedom. Give me all your money."

Cacambo approached the natives with the crumpled notes and handful of coins that represented all of Candide's fortune. But they seemed unimpressed and gesticulated fiercely. "What are they saying?" said Candide.

"They don't want it," said Cacambo. "We must barter: this is an unsophisticated market. It is no good offering these savages money, they would probably try to eat it! Open the backpack, we must offer them what we have!"

Candide drew out the remains of the ham and bread, and a bottle of water, and gave them to Cacambo, who again approached the natives. Candide once more watched as his friend remonstrated with them in a language he could not understand. He could follow, however, their expressions and wild gesticulations and feared for the worst. Cacambo returned, still carrying the provisions. "I told them that we were neither government soldiers, nor socialist rebels and offered them the food for goodwill," he said, "but all they want is for us to leave and promise not to return."

"We are offering to pay to go!" said Candide.

"I know," said Cacambo, "a strange place indeed. But let us not look such a gift-horse in the mouth. Let us go."

Candide was delighted not to be eaten alive,

and even more pleased at his discovery of such an innocent people. "A country where self-interest does not prevail," he thought as they made their way off. "What a pity we cannot stay longer. What a fortune I could have made!"

Chapter Seventeen

EL DORADO – I

"Well," said Cacambo to his master, when they had made good their departure, "this country is as dangerous as all the others. Take my advice and let us return to England by the shortest way."

"But how and by what way? If I return down river, I will be arrested and shot. If we stay here, we may at any moment be roasted on a spit. But how can I bring myself to leave that part of the world that contains Mistress Penelope."

"Let us make for the coast at Cayenne. We shall find ships there. Perhaps we can work our passage or find someone who will transport us out of the goodness of their heart."

Candide looked doubtful but agreed there was no better plan.

It was not easy to reach Cayenne. They knew more or less what direction to travel, but the way was barred by mountains, rivers, precipices, robbers and savages. Their provisions were exhausted and, for a month, they lived on wild fruit.

At length, they came to a stream bordered by coconut palms. The sight of these gave them new life and hope. Cacambo, who was as ready with advice as the old woman, said: "We are exhausted, and can walk no further. I can see an empty canoe; let us fill it with coconuts, embark and drift down with the current. A river always leads to some inhabited place. If we find nothing pleasant, at least we shall find something new."

"Agreed," said Candide, who was longing to be back in civilisation.

For a few miles, they were wafted between banks that were sometimes flowery, sometimes barren, sometimes level, sometimes rugged. The river gradually widened, then narrowed, until it reached a point where it disappeared into a tunnel beneath huge, terrifying crags. They decided to risk entering the tunnel, although the river carried them along with dreadful speed and noise.

Twenty-four hours later they again saw daylight, but just as they did so, their canoe was dashed to pieces on a reef. For almost a mile, they had to drag themselves from rock to rock. Then the ravine opened out upon an immense horizon, rimmed with inaccessible mountains.

The country appeared to be cultivated for beauty as much as for the production of crops, and everything which served the needs of man was pleasing to the sight. To their amazement, the roads were filled with carriages of lovely design and made of some glittering material, carrying men and women of remarkable good looks and drawn by big red horses, faster than the best horses of Europe or Arabia.

"Here is a country that beats England," said Candide.

They struck up from the river bank towards the first village they saw. Some village children, dressed in tattered gold brocade, were playing catch by the entrance. The two travellers noticed that the balls they threw and caught were coloured yellow, red and green, of remarkable brilliance. They were in fact coated with gold and studded with rubies and emeralds. They felt a strong desire to collect some of them: the smallest would have made the biggest ornament in the crown jewels.

"These children must be the sons of the king of this country," said Cacambo. At this moment the village teacher came to call the children back to their lessons. "There is the royal family's tutor," said Candide.

The urchins left their balls, and a number of other toys, lying on the ground. Candide picked them up and respectfully handed them to the teacher, indicating by signs that their Royal Highnesses had forgotten their gold and jewels. The teacher smiled, threw the objects down, glanced at Candide in surprise and followed the children back to the school.

The travellers carefully collected the treasures. "What a strange country!" said Candide. "The royal children here must be very properly educated, since they are taught not to imply intrinsic value to just metal and stones." They approached the first house in the village, which was built on the scale of a European palace. There was a crowd of people by the gate, and a great number inside. Delightful music, and a savoury smell of cooking, came from the house. Cacambo went up to the gate, and he heard people talking in Peruvian, which was his mother tongue.

"I will be your interpreter," he told Candide. "This is an inn; let us enter."

Two waiters, and two waitresses, all dressed in cloth of gold and wearing ribbons in their hair, invited them to sit down for the *plat de jour*. Dinner consisted of four different soups, garnished with the finest sweetmeats, a suckling pig weighing one hundred pounds, the most delicate white fish, and a number of delicious ragouts and tarts. The whole meal was served in dishes of a form of crystal glass. The waiters passed around liquors of various kinds, extracted from sugar cane, and a deep red wine of balance and sophistication.

Most of the company were pedlars and wagon drivers. They all had excellent manners: they asked Cacambo a few circumspect questions, and answered his questions willingly and fully.

After dinner, Candide deposited on the table two of the gold balls that they had picked up, thinking that these would amply pay for their meal. The landlord and landlady burst out laughing. "We can see that you are strangers here, gentlemen," said the landlord. "We are not accustomed to such, so you must pardon us for laughing when you offer to pay us with baubles picked up at the side of the road. No doubt you are not supplied with coins of this realm, but you need none to dine here. All inns established for the convenience of merchants and traders are paid for by the state. Anyway, you have dined ill here, because this is a poor village, but everywhere else you will be received more fittingly."

Cacambo translated the gist of this to Candide, whose surprise and bewilderment were as great as his valet's. "What sort of country is this," said Cacambo, "cut off from the rest of the world and yet so rich and so well ordered?"

"Probably the perfect market," said Candide, "for there must be such a country somewhere and, whatever Pangloss may have said, I have often perceived that the economy has great imperfections in England.

Chapter Eighteen

EL DORADO – II

Cacambo kept plying the landlord with questions, until the latter remarked: "I am a most ignorant man, and content to remain so. But we have here an old man, a former official at court, who is more learned, and also more communicative, than anyone else in the kingdom." He led Cacambo – accompanied by Candide, who was content to play second fiddle to his servant – to the old man's house.

It was a very modest dwelling, the door being only of silver, inlaid with gold, but was so elegantly wrought as to bear comparison with the most sumptuous. The hall was a plain affair of rubies and emeralds, but here too, good taste atoned for extreme simplicity.

The old man seated his visitors on a sofa

stuffed with humming-birds' feathers, had drinks brought to them in diamond goblets, and proceeded to satisfy their curiosity.

"I am one hundred and seventy-two years old," he said, "and my late father, who was equerry to the King, told me of the amazing revolutions he had witnessed in Peru. The kingdom in which you find yourself is the ancient country of the Incas, who very imprudently sallied from it to conquer another part of the world, and were themselves destroyed in the end by the Spanish.

"Some of the royal princes were wiser than the others, and remained in their native country. With the people's consent, they made a law that no inhabitant of our little kingdom should ever leave it. To this we owe the preservation of our innocence and happiness.

"The Spaniards had some confused knowledge of this country, which they called El Dorado, and an Englishman, a man called Raleigh, actually came very near it many years ago. But the unscalable rocks and precipices with which we are surrounded, have always hitherto sheltered us from the rapacity of the European nations, who have an unfathomable fondness for the pebbles and dirt of our land, for the sake of which they would kill us all to the last man." A long conversation followed, concerning the country's form of government, its customs, public spectacles and arts. Candide, with his taste for economics, asked through Cacambo how the country managed without trade.

The old man reddened a little. "Can you doubt that we could, and not be better for it?" he said. "The existence of nations makes trade a competition of politics and relative power, not economics. How would it be to our advantage to be paid so little for raw materials, and to pay so much for other people's finished goods? And one sight of our gold and silver and the idea of trade would be straight away forgotten."

"Is that sufficient reason for your good fortune?" asked Candide.

"Our children are taken from their parents at thirteen," said the old man, "and educated together centrally, to ensure that each reaches his or her full potential. They are allowed no free time, for we know that free time is the enemy of adolescence. We also pay no taxes, except those which are agreed locally, although sometimes they can be high."

Candide was delighted. "This is very different from England," he thought, "and also from Sir Charles' house. If friend Pangloss had ever seen El Dorado he would never have said that the manor was the finest thing on earth. There is nothing like seeing the world, that's certain."

At the end of the conversation, the old man put at the travellers' disposal a coach drawn by six horses, with twelve of his servants, to conduct them to court. "Excuse me," he said, "that my age deprives me of the honour of accompanying you. The King will receive you in a manner with which you will have no fault to find. If certain of the customs of the country do not please you, no doubt you will make allowances."

The six horses drew them at a great pace, and in less than four hours Candide and Cacambo arrived at the royal palace, which was on the outskirts of the capital. The road ahead was lined with tall, handsome buildings but the palace itself was an unostentatious affair. The façade itself was simple stone and there was none of the adornment and ceremony normally associated with great power. The king himself was dressed in simple clothes but he greeted them warmly and invited them to sup with him.

In the meantime they were shown the city. The public buildings seemed almost to touch the clouds. The market places were adorned with thousands of columns. Fountains of clear water, rose water and liquors played incessantly in the squares, which were paved with jewels and lined with sweet smelling flowers.

Candide asked to see the courts of justice and

the parliament. He learnt that there were no such things, and that there was no litigation in El Dorado. He asked if there were any prisons, and learnt that there were none. What surprised and pleased him more was the Palace of the Sciences, where he saw a great hall two hundred yards long, filled with mathematical and scientific instruments.

In the course of the whole afternoon, they saw perhaps a thousandth part of the city. They were then led back to the palace, where they sat down to table with His Majesty and several courtiers. The dinner was simple but excellent, and His Majesty a most entertaining host. Cacambo translated his jokes, which, as Candide noted with surprise, were witty even in translation.

They spent a month as the King's guests, and Candide began to get restive. "I admit," he said to Cacambo, "that the country where I was born is nothing to this place. But, when all's said, Mistress Penelope is not here, and you, too, doubtless have some loved one in Europe or elsewhere. If we remain here, we shall be only like the other inhabitants, whereas, if we return to our own world with but a dozen mules laden with the pebbles of El Dorado, we shall be richer than all the governments of Europe, we shall have nothing to fear from the police, and we may easily recover Mistress Penelope."

Cacambo agreed. The desire for freedom, to cut a figure amongst their own people, and to tell their travellers' tales, induced these fortunate beings to forsake their good fortune. They asked His Majesty for leave to depart.

"You are acting foolishly," said the King. "I know that my country is nothing very great. But when one is tolerably at ease in any place, one should remain there. I have, of course, no power to detain strangers: that would be an act of tyranny at variance both with our manner of life and with the code of our law. All men are free – go when you will.

"But you will not find it easy. It is impossible to ascend the swift river by which you miraculously came, or to pass through the rocky tunnel. The mountains entirely surrounding my kingdom are not climbable and the descent on the other side is barred by precipices.

"However, since you are so set on leaving us, I will ask our scientists to make a machine to help you on your journey. Once you are beyond the mountains, nobody can help you further. My subjects have taken a vow never to pass beyond our frontier, and are too wise to break it. Anything else you ask, you shall have."

"All we ask of Your Majesty," said Candide, "is a few mules laden with victuals, pebbles and the clay of your country."

"The King smile: "I cannot imagine what pleasure you Europeans find in our yellow clay. But take away as much as you will, and much good may it do you."

On the King's orders, his engineers made a machine to scale the mountain peaks and take these two extraordinary men out of the Kingdom. Candide and Cacambo were placed in the machine, together with two mules saddled and bridled for them to ride after they had crossed the mountains, twenty baggage mules laden with food and water, thirty carrying gifts of rich native workmanship, and fifty laden with gold, diamonds and other jewels.

When they and their mules had been ingeniously hoisted to the summit of the mountains, the engineers left them. Candide was filled with the thought of presenting his mules to Penelope. "Now we have the wherewithal to pay the Governor of Freetown," he said, "if Lady Penelope is to be had at any price whatsoever. Let us make for Cayenne and take ship there. Then let us decide which kingdom we shall purchase!"

Chapter Nineteen

THE SHIPMASTER

The first day's journey was pleasant, for the two travellers were heartened by the thought that they possessed more wealth than in all the countries of Europe combined. Deliciously daydreaming, Candide carved Penelope's name on trees.

On the second day, two of their mules were swallowed up in swamps, with their loads. Two more died of fatigue a few days later. Subsequently seven or eight starved to death in a desert, and some others fell down a precipice. After a while they had only two mules left.

"You see, my friend," Candide remarked to Cacambo, "how perishable are the riches of the world. Nothing really lasts except for virtue, and the bliss of again seeing Mistress Penelope."

"No doubt," said Cacambo. "But we still have two mules left with more treasure than the vaults of Zurich, and yonder I see a city. We are at the end of our troubles, and the beginning of our pleasures."

Near the city they found a local man lying on the ground. He wore only a pair of blue linen trousers, and his left leg and right arm had been cut off. "My God," said Candide, "what are you doing here, friend, in this deplorable condition?"

"I am waiting for my mother," said the man, "she can sometimes spare some food that she brings for me."

"But is it usual for your tribe to let you lie here in this condition?"

"No sir. My tribe used to farm all this land but the government sold it for a coffee plantation and my people were resettled many miles away. I was lucky enough to work clearing the forest, but as you can see, I met with an unfortunate accident in the process."

"But I cannot see any plantation," said Candide, looking to his right and left.

"No sir," said the native. "After the forest was cleared, the owners realised that they could save on transport costs with a different site nearer to market. But that is the price of your passion, sir, for coffee and for the lowest cost."

"Oh Pangloss," cried Candide. "You never guessed at such a nonsense! This is the end. I must renounce your view: the market does not always provide for the perfect allocation of resources."

"What does that mean?" said Cacambo.

"It is the madness of asserting that individuals left entirely to their own devices will act in their own interest so as to further the general good."

Candide looked again at the native, and burst into tears: thus, weeping, he entered the city.

They at once inquired if there was a ship in the harbour that could take them to Freetown. The person they spoke to was a Spanish shipmaster, who offered them reasonable terms, and made an appointment with them at an inn. Candide and Cacambo went there to wait for him, taking with them their two mules.

When they met, Candide, who always blurted out whatever was foremost in his mind, told the Spaniard all his adventures and disclosed his intention of carrying off Mistress Penelope.

"In that case, I would not dream of carrying you to Freetown," said the shipmaster. "I should be shot, and so should you. The fair Penelope is the Governor's favourite mistress."

Candide was aghast at this news, and wept for a long time. Then he took Cacambo aside. "I'll tell you what you must do, my dear friend," he said. "Each of us has in our pockets diamonds to the value of tens of millions. You are cleverer than me. Go to Freetown and rescue Mistress Penelope. If the Governor makes any difficulty, give him a million. If he holds out, give him two. You have not killed a general, so they have nothing against you.

"For my part, I shall get another ship and go to London, where I will wait for you. England is a free country, where we shall have nothing to fear from soldiers, rebels or savages."

Cacambo thoroughly agreed with this proposal. He was unhappy at parting from a good master, who had become a close friend, but the pleasure of doing him a service outweighed the grief of leaving him. He set out the same day, having been reminded by Candide not to forget the old woman. Cacambo was a very good man.

Candide spent some time longer in the city, waiting for another captain to carry him and his two remaining mules to England. He made all the preparations for a long voyage. At length a merchant who was master of a large vessel, offered his services.

"How much do you want," said Candide, "to carry me, my baggage and these two mules directly to London?" The shipmaster asked for ten thousand dollars, and Candide immediately agreed.

"Ho, ho!" thought the merchant, "this man must be very rich." A little while later he came back and said that the price had risen to twenty thousand dollars. "Very well, you shall have it." said Candide.

"Bless my soul," said the captain under his breath. Coming back a second time, he raised his price to thirty thousand dollars, pointing to the cost of fuel oil. "You shall have it," said Candide without hesitation.

"Ho, ho!" again thought the merchant, "thirty thousand dollars is nothing to this man. Those mules must certainly be laden with an immense treasure. I'll ask no more at present, but make him pay the first thirty thousand, and then we shall see."

Candide sold two small diamonds, the smaller of which was worth all the money that the shipmaster demanded, and paid him in advance. The two mules were put on board, and Candide took a small boat to join the ship in the harbour. The shipmaster seized his opportunity and sailed before Candide was half-way towards him.

Bewildered and stupefied, Candide soon lost sight of the ship. "Alas," he exclaimed, "this is a trick worthy of the world." Crushed with grief, he put back to the shore, having lost wealth beyond his dreams.

He went straight to the city magistrate. Being slightly agitated, he banged violently on the door, and in stating his case, spoke a little louder than was necessary. The magistrate fined him ten thousand for making too much noise, after which he listened patiently, promised to look into the matter as soon as the merchant returned, and charged another ten thousand for the costs of the hearing.

This behaviour reduced Candide to utter desperation. He had in his lifetime suffered worse misfortunes than this, but the cool impudence of the magistrate, coming on top of the villainy of the shipmaster, plunged him into a black melancholy. The wickedness of mankind presented itself nakedly before him, and he became obsessed with gloomy thoughts.

Shortly afterwards he learnt that a French ship was about to sail for Bordeaux. As he had no more mules laden with diamonds, he reserved a cabin at a reasonable price. He also advertised in the town that he would pay passage, board and two thousand dollars to any honest man who would accompany him on the voyage, a condition being that this man must be the most unfortunate, and the most dissatisfied with his lot, in the whole province.

The crowd of candidates who presented themselves was larger than a fleet of ships could carry. Seeking to narrow the field of choice, Candide selected about twenty men who seemed congenial, and invited them to dine with him at his inn. He stipulated that each of them should undertake to give a true account of his life, whilst Candide, for his part, promised to choose as his companion the man who seemed to him the most deserving of compassion, and the most justly dissatisfied with his lot. He also promised to give each of the others a small present.

The session lasted until four in the morning. Candide was reminded of what the old woman had said on the voyage up the river to Freetown, when she wagered that every single person on board the ship had suffered great misfortunes. As each story was told, he thought to himself: "Pangloss would be hard put to it now to maintain his favourite thesis. For sure, if there is any place where people like this do not have need of help and support, it can only be in El Dorado, and nowhere else on earth."

Candide finally decided in favour of a poor teacher who had spent much of his life in advertising – no employment, he reflected could be more artificial than this. This teacher (who was, as it happened, a very good sort of man) had lost all his money in a commodity pyramid scheme and was now too poor to seek restitution through the courts.

It must be admitted that all the other candidates were at least as unfortunate as this one. Candide's real reason for choosing him was a hope that, being a well-read man, he would relieve the tedium of the voyage. The other candidates all thought that Candide was doing them an injustice, but he appeased them by giving each a thousand dollars.

Chapter Twenty

MARTIN THE CONTRARIAN

Candide and the old teacher, whose name was Martin, had both seen and suffered so much that even if the ship had been sailing to China via the Cape of Good Hope, the subjects of economics and society could still have kept them busy talking throughout the voyage.

Candide, however, had one great advantage over Martin: he still hoped to see Penelope again, whereas Martin had nothing to look forward to. Moreover, Candide still had money and jewels. True, he had lost eighty mules laden with the world's greatest treasure, and he was still vexed by the roguery of the merchant who had stolen his fortune, nevertheless, when he thought of what he still had in his pockets, or spoke of Penelope – and especially after a good dinner – he continued to incline towards the doctrines of Pangloss.

"Tell me, Mr Martin," he said, "what is your opinion of the matter? Do you not agree that it is only the imperfections in the market that prevent the best possible allocation of resources and inflict such misery on individuals?"

"Sir," said Martin, "I believe that there can be no equality in society without some form of intervention."

"Surely you are jesting? No one believes in such a thing nowadays."

"That is my view, I cannot help it. I can hold no other belief."

"You must be mad," said Candide. "Why, intervention distorts the market and harms the very people it is supposed to help."

"The problem is this," replied Martin eventually. "What you say is true by definition. Western economics works because it sets as the goal of society an ever-increasing standard of living measured purely in terms of increasing consumption. The unfettered market is undeniably best suited to producing more and more consumer goods. But if you change the goal of society – for example to the reduction of inequality or, say, the reduction of crime – then the requirement for more and more products is less important, even counter-productive."

"But the market provides the best possible allocation of resources," said Candide. "How can it benefit society to interfere with that?"

"I do not agree," said Martin. "The free market provides one of many possible allocations of resources. As soon as you say that it is the best, you are making an ethical judgement about the goals and aims of your society. The wisdom or otherwise of that judgement should be debated, not within the confines of economics as we understand it, for the answer will be tautological, but in the realms of ethics and morals. That is why our grandfathers called the science 'Political Economy' – they knew better than to pretend its values were neutral."

Candide did not accept this argument. He knew that state intervention encouraged dependency and was a cause of poverty, not its cure.

"My dear friend," he said, "the perfect allocation of resources is not a thing of chance. It is regulated by the price mechanism and reflects people's appreciation of value, and the relative costs of supply. It is the servant of society, not its master. And there is no better way of rationing the world's scarce resources."

"We can disagree about the last point," said the teacher. "But, Candide, your values are as much culturally determined as your economics.

Isolated from your society you would not for long value gold above food!"

"But that is supply and demand. The law of diminishing marginal returns…."

"Is simply determined by what you have been taught to value and the manner you have been led to behave."

In the midst of this discussion, they spied a freighter coming towards them. As it drew closer, Candide realised that it was the same ship he had last seen disappearing over the horizon with his mules on board. As it pulled alongside, the shipmaster's deputy came on board with one of Candide's mules. "Sir, I am deeply sorry," said this good man, "that you were tricked in such a fashion. When the crime was uncovered, the captain escaped in a small boat and we put about to look for you. The rogue has escaped with one of your mules, but here is the other, safe and well."

Candide felt more joy at the recovery of this one animal than the grief he had felt at losing eighty of them, all laden with the treasure of El Dorado.

"You see," said Candide, "there is a place for honesty in this world. That man certainly did not have to bring my mule back to me."

"What has honesty to do with the market?" said Martin. "Good and bad pre-date the economy.

Economic relations are the superstructure, not the foundation."

The ship continued its voyage, and Candide and Martin continued their discussions. They argued for a fortnight, at the end of which they were as far advanced as at the beginning. However, the main thing was that they conversed, and in the exchange of ideas and the company of each other, found consolation for their grief.

Candide frequently embraced his mule. "Since I have found you," he said to it, "I may well find Penelope also."

Chapter Twenty-One

THE NATURE OF MANKIND

"Have you ever been to France, Mr Martin?" asked Candide. They were within sight of the coast.

"Yes, I have passed through several of its provinces. The inhabitants are the same as in the rest of the world. Half of them are mad, others too clever, or too simple. Still others affect to be witty. For all, however, the chief occupation is making love, the second is slander, and the third is talking nonsense."

"But have you been to Paris, Mr Martin?"

"Yes, I have been there, and it contains all the kinds of people I have mentioned. It is like any big city: a chaos where everyone seeks pleasure, or advancement, and as far as I can make out, scarcely anyone finds either.

"As soon as I had arrived there, I had my wallet taken by a pick-pocket in St. Germain. I myself was arrested as a thief, and imprisoned. Afterwards I worked as a copy-writer for a great firm. I came to know the whole pack of chancers, liars and charlatans. Some of the people are said to be very polite, but I never met them."

"For my part," said Candide, "I have no wish particularly to go to France. As you can imagine, after spending a month in El Dorado, there is nothing else on earth that I wish to see – excepting Mistress Penelope. I am going to wait for her in London, and will pass through France on my way to England. Will you come with me?"

"Gladly. I have heard that life in London is pleasant only for the rich, but that visitors who have plenty of money are very well received there also. I have none, but you have, so I shall follow you wherever you please."

"While we are on the subject, do you believe that man is intrinsically good, to be encouraged and gently guided, or fundamentally bad, to be restrained and controlled?"

"Both."

"And do you think that men have always slaughtered one another? Have they always been liars, cheats, traitors, robbers, deceivers, cowards, enviers, gluttons, drunkards, misers, sycophants, slanderers, debauchees, fanatics, hypocrites and fools?"

"Do you think that foxes have always devoured rabbits at every opportunity?"

"Doubtless."

"Well if foxes have always been the same, why should men have altered?"

"Ah, but there is a great difference, for free will…."

They were still arguing when they arrived in Bordeaux.

Chapter Twenty-Two

A RICH STRANGER IN PARIS

Candide stayed in Bordeaux only long enough to sell a few pebbles from El Dorado, and to procure a good vehicle with room for both their baggage. He now found the philosopher Martin's company indispensable. He was distressed, however, at having to part with his mule, which he gave to a model farm.

It struck Candide that all the travellers they met at inns along the road told him that they were going to Paris. This general eagerness to go there, at length, made him wish to see the city, which was not much out of the way to London.

He entered a poor quarter, not much better than some of the cities he had seen on his travels. On putting up at an inn, he was overtaken by a slight illness, caused by fatigue. Since he had a huge ring on his finger and a strong-box amongst his luggage he was immediately attended to by two doctors, whom he had not asked for, by a number of close friends who came to sit by his bedside, and by two devoted ladies, who kept ordering cups of broth for him.

"I, too, have been ill in a big city," said Martin, "but I was very poor, and had no friends, nurses or doctors. I recovered quickly."

As a result of the application of various drugs and medicines, Candide's illness became serious. A priest came and offered to say prayers for him, would he but make a donation to his church and to his charity. Candide refused the transaction and Martin offered to throw the priest out. The priest swore that Candide would not receive burial. Martin swore that he just might bury the priest. After a heated argument, the priest was shown the door.

Candide recovered. During his convalescence a number of his attentive companions regularly came and dined with him. They played cards for high stakes. Candide was surprised to find that he never held any aces; this did not surprise Martin.

Amongst Candide's new friends was a travelling salesman from Lyons; one of those obsequious, quick-witted, obliging, impudent, fawning, useful creatures who lie in wait for passing strangers. He overheard some of Candide and Martin's conversation and offered to take them to a lecture to be given that evening at the Acadamie Française. The speaker, a noted politician, argued against the hegemony of market economics.

"Taken to its origins," he said, "the market has its roots not in rational and efficient exchange by specialists, the myth of the butcher and the baker and the blacksmith, but in individual insufficiency and human need. Man must both want something and lack it, to enter the market. It may well be that a lower standard of living is preferable if it brings psychological and emotional security."

Candide listened attentively to these remarks and, although he did not agree with all that was said, he formed a high opinion of the speaker. He leaned over to the salesman and asked in a whisper who this excellent speaker was.

"He is a man of letters," said the salesman. "He is the most honest politician in the country and never promises what the country cannot afford. Hence he is never elected."

"A truly great man," said Candide, "a second Pangloss!" Then, addressing the gentleman himself: "Sir," he said, "I take it that you are of the opinion that the market, for all its faults, provides the best possible allocation of resources within an economic system, and that economic liberties are at the root of social freedom and equality?"

"*I*, sir? I think no such thing! I find that those who support a free market are generally just expressing their satisfaction with the current distribution of wealth and power. To argue that everyone competes equally is like pitting a giant against a dwarf, and claiming that the fight is fair because the ring is flat. The truly free market sets all against all in a frenzy from which there is no escape. There is no association that it does not seek to break, no link that it would not destroy."

"I have seen worse things than those you mention," said Candide. "Yet a learned man, who has since had the misfortune to be hanged, taught me that these evils are mere shadows in a beautiful picture."

"Your friend had his joke at the world's expense," said Martin. "These shadows, as you call them, are horrible blemishes."

"These blemishes do not exist in theory. They are the imperfections, not the thing itself."

"But then the imperfections are the point. We must live with them."

They continued their discussion back at the inn. Martin and the scholar talked, whilst Candide fell into conversation with a French lady, to whom he told about his travels. After supper, the lady took Candide to her bedroom, where she sat him on a sofa. "Well," she said, "are you still so violently fond of Mistress Penelope of Market Morton in the county of Sussex?"

"Yes, madam."

The lady smiled affectionately. "You answer like an Englishman. A Frenchman would have said: "It is true that I loved Mistress Penelope. But since I have seen you, I fear that I love her no longer."

"Alas, madam, I will make what answer you please."

"You fell in love with her, I am told, when you picked up her handkerchief. You shall pick up my garter."

"Most willingly, madam," Candide did so.

"And now you must put it on again." Candide did this too.

"Young man, you are a stranger here. I make some of my Parisian lovers languish for a whole fortnight, but I will surrender to you the first night, as my patriotic duty towards a young man from England."

Whilst speaking, the beautiful lady noticed that the young foreigner was wearing two enormous gold rings. She praised them with such unaffected enthusiasm that they were soon transferred from Candide's fingers to hers.

As he rejoined Martin and the salesman, Candide felt some remorse at having been unfaithful to Penelope. The salesman, too, was dissatisfied. He had received only a small share so far of Candide's losses at cards – not to mention the two gold rings – and he began to plan how to turn his acquaintance with Candide to the greatest possible profit.

He began talking about Penelope, and Candide remarked that when he saw her again, he would humbly ask her pardon for his unfaithfulness. The salesman listened with courteous attention. He seemed to take a keen interest in everything that Candide said, did, or planned to do.

"And so, sir, you have an engagement in London?"

"Yes. I absolutely must find Mistress Penelope." Carried away by the pleasure of talking of his beloved, Candide related, as he so often did, some of his adventures with that illustrious Sussex damsel.

"I suppose," said the salesman, "that Mistress Penelope has a great deal of wit, and writes charming letters?"

"I have never received any from her. For you must remember that, having been driven out of the mansion for my love of her, I could not write to her, and soon afterwards I learnt that she was dead. I then found her and lost her again, and now I have sent a messenger to her, nearly five thousand miles away, and I am waiting for her answer."

The salesman listened attentively and seemed pensive. Soon afterwards he cordially embraced Candide and Martin, and left them.

The next morning Candide received the following letter:

"My dearest Love, for the last week I have been in this very city, confined by illness. I have learnt that you are here, and would fly to your arms, were I able to stir. I learnt of your arrival when I was in Bordeaux, where I have left the faithful Cacambo and the old woman. They will soon follow me. The Governor of Freetown has taken everything from me but your heart. Come to me: your presence will either give me new life, or kill me with pleasure."

Torn between joy at this charming and unexpected letter and grief at the news of Penelope's illness, Candide took his gold and diamonds and found a guide to lead Martin and himself to the hotel where she was lodging. When he entered her room, he trembled, his heart beat violently, and his voice quavered. He started to pull back the curtains and look for the light.

"Beware of doing that, sir!" said the

chambermaid. "The Mistress cannot bear the light." She quickly pulled the curtains closed again.

"Dearest Penelope," sobbed Candide, "how are you faring? If you cannot see me, speak to me, at least."

"She cannot speak," said the maid.

He produced a purse of gold and was about to move to the bed when the door opened and a police officer entered the room, followed by the salesman and a squad of men.

"Are these the suspects?" he asked, and gave orders that they should be arrested and taken to prison.

"Travellers are not treated like this in El Dorado," said Candide.

"This makes me even more contrarian," said Martin.

"Where are you taking us, officer?"

"To prison."

Martin collected his wits and realised that the pretend Penelope and the salesman were frauds, and that the officer could easily be got rid of. He enlightened Candide, and the latter, in his impatience to find the true Penelope, immediately offered the officer a bribe of three small diamonds, worth about three thousand dollars each.

"Ah, sir," said the man, "had you committed

ever so many crimes, you would still be the best man living! Three diamonds, worth thousands and thousands, I'll be bound! Why sir, far from carrying you to jail, I would escort you to wherever you want to go."

"We are trying to reach London."

"Why, I have a brother at Dieppe, in Normandy. I will conduct you to him, and if you have a diamond for him as well, I am sure he will take as much care of you as I myself should."

He ordered Candide and Martin's handcuffs removed, told his men that a mistake had been made, and dismissed them. He then brought Candide and Martin to Dieppe, where he left them in the care of his brother.

There was a small ship in the harbour, and the officer's brother, whose devoted loyalty had been purchased for three more diamonds, put Candide and Martin aboard it. The ship was about to sail to Portsmouth rather than London, but Candide did not care. He felt that he had escaped from hell, and reckoned on resuming his journey to London as soon as possible.

Chapter Twenty-Three

"TO ENCOURAGE THE OTHERS"

"Ah Pangloss, Pangloss! Ah, Martin, Martin! Ah, dearest Penelope – what sort of a world is this?" sighed Candide.

"Something utterly mad and abominable." said Martin.

"Have you been to England? Do you think we are as mad there as everywhere else?"

"I think it is an extreme form of madness, where fondness for naked wealth and consumption have replaced all decent behaviour, where neither the government nor charity will provide for the weak and disadvantaged."

On shore, a crowd of people surrounded a courtroom. A man emerged covered in a blanket and held at each arm by a policeman. The crowd shouted and tried to reach the man, banging their fists on the side of the van into which he was bundled.

"What is all this?" said Candide, "what demons have run amok here?" He enquired who the man was. "A man who has abused children," he was told.

Candide expressed his disgust at this most unnatural of crimes. "I assume that if he is guilty he will be sent to prison for many hundreds of years," he said.

"Seven," was the reply.

"But I read only yesterday of a fraudster, an American, who has been sent to jail for one hundred and fifty years!"

"Yes," said Martin, "but he has lost a lot of important people a lot of money. His penalty must be exemplary to encourage others in a similar position not to do the same thing and suffer such losses."

Candide was shocked. He determined not to waste time by landing in Portsmouth and struck a bargain with the boat's captain to take him directly to London.

They sailed along the coast, through the straights of Dover, and arrived at London. "God be praised!" said Candide, embracing Martin. "Here I shall see Penelope again. I trust Cacambo as I trust myself. Everything will work out fine!"

Chapter Twenty-Four

PAQUETTE AND THE BANKER

In London, Candide looked for Cacambo at every inn and coffee-house, and among all the ladies of pleasure, but could not find him. He sent every day to inquire what ships had come in; but still no news of Cacambo.

"What!" he said to Martin. "Have I had time to travel from Cayenne to Bordeaux, then to Paris, to Dieppe, Portsmouth and now to spend some months in London – and still Penelope has not arrived? All that I have found in her place has been a female trickster. Penelope is certainly dead, and I have nothing to do but to follow her.

"Alas, how much better it would have been to remain in the paradise of El Dorado, than to have returned to this cursed Europe! You are right, my dear Martin: there is nothing but misery and greed in this wicked world."

He fell into a black melancholy, and took no part in the delights and temptations of the busy city. Not one lady paid the least attention to him.

"Upon my word," said Martin, "you are very simple to imagine that a poor-bred valet, with five or six million in his pocket, would go to the end of the world in search of your mistress and bring her to you in London. If he finds her, he will keep her for himself. If he does not find her, he will take another. I advise you to forget Cacambo, and your mistress, too."

Martin was no comfort. Candide's melancholy grew, whilst Martin continued to demonstrate to him that there was very little virtue or happiness on earth – except possibly in El Dorado, where nobody could go.

One day Candide saw in Trafalgar Square a young well-dressed man, with his arm around a girl. The man, a banker, was clear complexioned, bright-eyed and vigorous, with an assured manner and a bold and spirited presence. The girl, who was very pretty, was laughing. Now and then she glanced adoringly at her lover, and stroked his hands.

"You will allow," said Candide to Martin, "that there, at least, are two happy people. Everywhere, hitherto – except in El Dorado – I have met only the unfortunate. But as to this couple, I am prepared to bet they are most happy creatures."

"I'll wager they are not."

"Well, we have only to ask them to dine with us, and you will see whether I am mistaken."

Candide then accosted the couple, and invited them to come to dinner with him and Martin at his hotel.

The banker accepted the invitation. The girl blushed and followed unwillingly, repeatedly staring at Candide with an air of surprise and embarrassment, her eyes full of tears. When they reached the hotel, the banker excused himself to take a call, and the others sat down to dinner. The girl said to him: "How, Master Candide, do you not recognise Paquette?"

Candide had not before looked at her very closely, since he cared for no woman but Penelope. "Ah, my poor child!" he now exclaimed. "Is it you? And was it you who reduced Dr Pangloss to that fine condition in which I saw him?"

"Alas, yes sir, it is I, indeed, and I see that you know everything. I have learnt of the dreadful misfortunes that have befallen the whole household of Lady Rathbone and Mistress Penelope. I promise you my own lot has been scarcely less pitiful.

"I was a good girl when you saw me last, but innocent. Too innocent to take precautions during Dr Pangloss' private tutorials. The consequences were terrible and I was obliged to leave the house, only a little while after Sir Charles had kicked you out. A doctor took pity on me and performed the operation. Out of gratitude, I lived with him for some time as a servant and became his mistress. His wife suspected and became ragingly jealous. She was a fury! The doctor was the ugliest man alive and I was the unhappiest of creatures.

"You will know, sir, how dangerous it can be for a jealous wife to be married to a doctor. Incensed at his wife's behaviour, he took the opportunity one day when she had a slight cold, and gave her a medicine that was so effective that she died within two hours, in frightful convulsions.

"The police brought criminal charges against the doctor and I was accused of being an accomplice. My innocence would not have saved me, had I not been tolerably pretty. The judge set me free, on condition that he should succeed the doctor in my affections. But I was soon supplanted by a rival, turned out without a penny, and obliged to take to the abominable trade which you men think so pleasing, but which to us is nothing but a bottomless pit of misery.

"So I came to walk the streets in London. Sir,

if only you knew what it is like to have to sleep with every sort of man, to be exposed to their insults and outrages, to beg for clothing and food, to be robbed by one man of what one has earned from another, to have to pay bribes to the police, and to have no real prospect but a hideous old age or an early death. Did you but know all this, you would conclude that I am one of the unhappiest people alive."

"You see," said Martin, "I have won half of our bet already."

"But you seemed so gay and content when I met you," Candide said to Paquette. "You laughed, you stroked that banker's hands with such genuine fondness that I thought you to be as happy as – so it now appears – you are, in truth, wretched."

"Ah sir, that is one of the miseries of the trade. Yesterday I was beaten by a senior civil servant; today I must seem merry to please a banker."

Candide had heard enough; he admitted that Martin had won his wager – at least, as far as Paquette was concerned. The banker joined them for dinner.

The meal was a pleasant one, and towards the end they were talking freely. "You seem an enviable man," said Candide. "Your face glows with healthiness, you have a pretty girl on your arm, your wealth is evident: you must be very content."

"I wish it was so," he replied, "but I take no great pride in my work. I have no time to enjoy my money, and my workplace is full of jealousy and discord. My heart sinks every morning as I wake up and remember what I must face each day."

"Well," said Martin, "I think I have now won the bet entirely."

Candide gave two thousand pounds to Paquette. "With this money, at least she now will be happy."

"I doubt it. It will probably make her more wretched still once it is spent."

"Be that as it may, one thing comforts me. I see that one often meets people whom one had never expected to meet again. I found my lost mule, and now Paquette. It may well be that I shall also find Penelope."

"Indeed, I wish that one day she may bring you happiness, but I much doubt it."

"You are very harsh."

"I have seen the world."

"See the people in the street. Certainly at least some of them look happy."

"If you could see them at home or on their own, you would see the cares that weigh on them. The very rich have their worries; ordinary people have theirs too. It is true that, in the main, the lot of the ordinary man is preferable to that of the very rich, but the difference is not great."

"There is talk of a certain philosopher called Lord Pocurant, who lives in a fine house in the city. He is said to be a man who has never known grief."

"I should be glad to meet such an extraordinary being."

Candide thereupon sent a message to Lord Pocurant, asking for permission to visit him next day.

Chapter Twenty-Five

LORD POCURANT

Candide and Martin hired a taxi and were taken to Lord Pocurant's mansion. Its gardens were extensive and were adorned with fine marble statues, and the house itself was of great beauty. The master of the house, a man of about sixty, and very rich, received the two sightseers civilly, but without much ceremony. Candide was a little disconcerted by this, but Martin was rather pleased.

They walked down a long hallway. Candide paused at the door of a room which was padlocked. Through a small window he could see rows of computers, now clearly disused and covered with dust. "Are those machines out of date?" he asked their host. "I think that they always were," said his Lordship. "I spent many years in that room trying to refine ever more complicated models of the economy, to predict better the future movement of commodity prices. Eventually, I found that I could get better results by sticking pins in a chart, blindfold! The real world, I am pleased to say, is infinitely too complicated for such imitation."

After coffee, they walked along a large gallery. Candide admired the pictures. One in particular caught his eye: a portrait of a distinguished looking man in eighteenth century clothes. Candide asked who it was. "Do you not recognise Adam Smith?" said Pocurant, "The father of economics?"

Candide apologised and said that he was, of course, very familiar with his work. "No doubt, sir," he said, "he is a great hero of yours?"

"I am sorry, he is not," Pocurant replied. "It was he who first propagated this idea that each man's self-interest, taken together, combines to serve the general good. He may have been a first-rate economist, but he was a fifth-rate observer of human nature."

"But the invisible hand…." began Candide.

"The only thing invisible in Adam Smith," said Pocurant, "is any sign that he understood what motivates men!"

Candide argued against these sentiments, but only a little and with discretion. Martin was in full agreement with them.

After an excellent lunch, they repaired to the library, where Candide noticed the collected works of David Ricardo, magnificently bound, and complimented his host on his taste. "This book," he said, "was once the delight of the great Pangloss, another great economist."

"It is no delight to me," said Pocurant. "At one time I was made to believe that I took pleasure in it. At least he attempts to systemize, which is better than the mess of Smith. But 'the factors of production'? It is transparently an attempt to justify the ownership of land."

"Perhaps your Lordship prefers the work of Marx?" said Candide.

"I suppose at least Marx seemed to sense that something was wrong," he said. "But the edifice is unsustainable. It is not surprising, I suppose. Ultimately, it is a view from the heart, and you cannot use the language and concepts of liberal economics to negate liberal economics itself."

Candide, who had been brought up never to form an opinion of his own, was astonished by all this. Martin, however, thought Pocurant's attitude very reasonable.

"And here is Lenin," said Candide, turning to another shelf. "Surely, you do not advocate a centrally planned economy?"

"No, certainly not," said Pocurant. "Think

how inefficient a large company can become: duplication of effort, multiplication of unnecessary roles, scores of middle-management devoted to the avoidance of error, empire-building and destructive politicking. Imagine the whole country as just one company: it just doesn't bear thinking about!

"And it takes the heart out of human nature. Every man and woman wants to do better, for themselves and for their children. That is no crime; it is the most basic instinct.

"Mind you, at least they knew that the economy was a political being. Non-intervention is as much a political decision as intervention, and the results are political in nature."

"You sound as if you would admire Keynes," said Candide, scanning the walls for The General Theory.

"I do not allow that book in this house," said Pocurant. "How can you build a theory on 'equilibriums' in a world that is infinitely different from every second to the next?"

Candide was grieved, for he had great respect for Adam Smith, and was rather fond of Keynes. "Alas," he whispered to Martin, "I fear that this man must hold our current economists in great contempt."

"There would be no great harm in that," said Martin.

"What a superior being!" Candide muttered between his teeth. "What a great genius must be this Pocurant! No great man is good enough for him!"

When the two sightseers had taken their leave of His Lordship, Candide remarked to Martin: "Well, I think that we have found the happiest of mortals – he thinks himself superior to all that is past."

"But is there pleasure in condemning everyone and everything, in perceiving faults where others have seen only geniuses?"

"Well, it seems that the only really happy man will be me, when I see Penelope again."

But the days and weeks passed by, with no news of Cacambo. Candide was so overwhelmed with grief that he did not even notice the ingratitude of Paquette, who never came to visit him.

Chapter Twenty-Six

SUPPER WITH SIX PRESIDENTS

Candide, Martin and the other guests at the hotel were just going in to dinner, when a man with a large beard came up behind Candide, took him by the arm, and said: "Hold yourself ready to leave with us; do not fail."

It was Cacambo. Almost beside himself with joy, Candide embraced his dear friend. "Penelope must be here too, I suppose?" he said. "Where is she? Lead me to her, so that I may die of joy in her presence!"

"Penelope is not here," said Cacambo. "She is in Istanbul."

"Good heavens, Istanbul! But no matter – if she were in China, I would fly thither. Let us be gone!"

"We will go after supper. I can say no more to

you now. I must go and attend to my boss who sits at that table. But say not a word, only eat your supper and hold yourself ready."

In a turmoil of emotions – delight to have met his faithful agent again, astonishment to find him in the employ of someone else, obsessed with the prospect of recovering his mistress – Candide sat down to supper. At the table with him were Martin, who had listened unemotionally to his conversation with Cacambo, and six strangers recently arrived in London.

Cacambo, who sat behind one of these strangers, leaned forward towards the end of the meal and said: "Mr President, you can go when you please, the car is ready." After saying this, he left the room. The other guests looked at each other in surprise, but said nothing.

Another man approached one of the other diners. "Mr President, your car is at Westminster. Your wife will meet us there." He, too, then withdrew.

The surprise of the company grew. A third attendant went up to a third of the strangers, and said: "Mr President, sir, we should not stay much longer. I will go and get everything ready." The attendant also immediately went out.

Candide and Martin took it for granted that these people were characters in some form of charade. A fourth attendant said to the fourth stranger: "Mr President, we can leave as soon as you are ready," and also went out. A fifth man said the same to the fifth attendant. A sixth man, however, whose boss sat next to Candide, made a different remark: "I am sorry Mr President, but I can no longer trust you. We may both be sent to jail this very night. I am going to make my own arrangements. Farewell."

The six strangers, Candide and Martin sat in deep silence, until Candide broke it. "Gentlemen," he said, "this is very droll. How come you all to be presidents? I must confess that my friend Martin and I are just common citizens."

Cacambo's boss answered gravely: "I am not joking. I am the ex-president of a small republic in the Indian Ocean where I led a centre-left government committed to a system of private enterprise within a framework of governmental intervention and regulation. I have come to London to promote a book on the injustices of the colonial era."

The man next to him spoke next: "I was the leader of a small Caribbean island. We were slightly to the left of the centre-left, and were committed to welfare support and equality of opportunity for all. I am in London to promote my book on social injustice and poverty."

A third said: "My country could not afford the luxuries these men have described. We operated a free-market economy, albeit with appropriate safety nets for the sick and the unemployed. I am in London to find a publisher for my book on the dangers of socialism in the Indian Ocean and the Caribbean."

The fourth said: "I was the President of Ruritania and we were committed to the state ownership of all the means of production, distribution and exchange. My people knew, however, that the closest we would get in practice was a form of social democratic pragmatism but they still drew inspiration from our lofty ideals. I too have come to London to promote my book on the dangers of militantism, and the influence of my father on my early life."

The fifth said "I too have been President of Ruritania. I have twice lost control of the country, once in a coup followed by an election, and once in an election followed by a coup. I am now resigned to opposition and live in London and Geneva. I am working on my memoirs but the distractions are many."

The sixth president said: "Gentlemen, I am not so grand a person as any of you. I once was president of a great country, the foremost in its continent. But the winds of change blew all that away and we know our time is past. I am wanted in my own country and have come to London to seek protection under international law, but the processes are slow and not without risk and great expense."

This last utterance filled the five other presidents with noble compassion, and they each gave him tokens of their esteem and promises of diplomatic protection. Candide gave him a diamond worth twenty thousand pounds.

"Who is this man," said one of the presidents, "who is able to give such a gift to a stranger. Are you also a successful politician, sir?"

"No sir," said Candide, "and I do not wish to be."

As they were leaving the table, four ambassadors from the Middle East came in. They had come to London to argue for trade concessions, and for help in keeping up the price of oil. But Candide paid no attention to these newcomers: all that he cared about was to go to Istanbul in search of Penelope.

Chapter Twenty-Seven

JOURNEY TO ISTANBUL

Cacambo had reserved seats for Candide and Martin on the Turkish Airlines flight that was to carry his boss back to the Indian Ocean via Istanbul. After presenting themselves again to the President, they boarded the plane.

"How strange to eat with six presidents," said Candide, as they made their way on board, "and one so poor that I gave him charity! Perhaps there are many other politicians still more unfortunate.

"For my part, I have lost only eighty mules laden with treasure, and am now flying to the arms of Penelope. I say it once more, my dear Martin, Pangloss was right – we do live in a perfect world."

"I hope you are right."

"But truly, was that not an improbable

adventure? Never before has it been heard of for six presidents to dine together at an hotel."

"It is not more extraordinary than most of the things that have happened to us. There are many countries in the world, most have a president and there are plenty of ex-presidents. As for us having the honour of supping with six of them, it is a mere trifle, unworthy of note. What does it matter with whom one dines, so long as the fare is good?"

On board the plane, Candide fell on the neck of his old friend Cacambo. "What news of Penelope?" he said. "Is she still a paragon of beauty? Does she still love me? How is she? You have doubtless purchased for her the finest house in Istanbul."

"My dear Candide, Penelope washes dishes in a small restaurant in a run-down quarter of town. The owner pays her only five dollars a day but she is an illegal immigrant so cannot complain. What is worse, she has lost her beauty and has grown very ugly."

"Ugly or pretty, I am a man of honour, and am bound to love her always. But how can she have been reduced to such an abject condition, with the five or six millions that you brought to her?"

"I will tell you. First, I was obliged to give two millions to Senor Don Fernando d'Ibarro y

Figueroa y Mascarenes for his permission to take Mistress Penelope away with me. Then pirates stripped us of the rest and we ended up on an island in the Indian Ocean. The old woman worked as a housekeeper and I am in the employ of the ex-president, as you have heard. Penelope could find no work and was sent to Istanbul by the brother of the owner of the restaurant in which she now labours, as was the old woman."

"What a chain of disasters! But, after all, I still have some diamonds left. I can easily rescue Penelope…. It is a pity that she is grown ugly."

"What think you?" Candide continued, speaking now to Martin. "Who is most to be pitied: any of the presidents we have met, or I?"

"I cannot tell. To find the answer, I would have to enter into all your hearts."

"Ah, if Pangloss were here, he would know the answer, and would tell us it."

"I do not know by what measure your Pangloss can weigh human misfortunes. I suppose, however, that there are millions of men on earth who are a hundred times more to be pitied that any of those politicians."

"That may well be."

Once they reached Istanbul, Candide paid a heavy price to release Cacambo from his service. They and Martin set off into the city. However ugly Penelope might have become, Candide was resolved to find her.

Two tramps sat at the back of the bus. Candide noticed them especially, as he felt sorry for them. Their disfigured features seemed rather like those of Pangloss and the unlucky camp commandant, Penelope's brother. The resemblance touched and saddened Candide, and he looked at the two men still more attentively. "In truth," he said to Cacambo, "if I had not seen Master Pangloss hanged, and I, the misfortune to kill Penelope's brother, the commandant, I should believe that these two tramps were they."

On hearing the words "Pangloss" and "the commandant", the two tramps uttered a cry and rushed towards them. "Why, it is Candide!" they exclaimed.

"Am I dreaming?" said Candide. "Am I awake? Can this be real? Is this Penelope's brother, whom I killed? And Master Pangloss, whom I saw hanged?"

"Yes; it is us, it is us!"

"What, is this the great economist?" said Martin.

Candide embraced the commandant and Pangloss again and again. "And how is it, my dear sir, that I did not kill you? And you, my dear Pangloss, how have you come to life again after being hanged? And why are you both here, and in this condition?"

"Is it true that my dear sister is in this country? Can this really be my dear Candide?" asked the brother and Pangloss.

"Yes it is," said Candide to both questions. He introduced Martin and Cacambo to the two others, and there were embraces and loud conversation all round.

They reached the centre of the city and Candide sold a diamond for ten thousand dollars, although it was worth double that amount, and Pangloss and the commandant were soon fed, washed and dressed anew. The former flung himself weeping at the feet of his benefactor, whilst the latter nodded his thanks, and promised to return the money at the first opportunity.

"But is it possible," the commandant asked, "that my sister should be in Turkey?"

"It is more than possible: it is certain," said Candide. "She is scouring the dishes in a restaurant not far from here."

Two more diamonds were sold, and they all set out to rescue Penelope.

Chapter Twenty-Eight

THE TRAMPS' STORIES

"Once again, I must ask your pardon," said Candide to Penelope's brother, "for shooting you through the heart."

"Let us say no more about it. I must admit that I myself acted a little hastily. But since you wish to know by what accident I come to be here, I will tell you.

"The camp surgeon cured me of the wound you gave me. Some time afterwards we were attacked and I was taken prisoner by the government forces, who imprisoned me in Freetown, just after my sister had left that city.

After peace was declared, I returned to Peru and was sent as an aide to the ambassador here in Istanbul.

"I had not been a week in my new position

when I met a very handsome young office-boy. The weather was hot and the young man had an inclination to bathe. I took the opportunity to do likewise. I did not know that it was a crime for two men to be found naked in such circumstances. I was dismissed without a penny and found myself on the streets thereafter.

"But now I would like to know, how come my sister to be working in the kitchens of a restaurant here in Istanbul?"

"And you, my dear Pangloss," said Candide, "how is it that I see you again?"

"You saw me hanged, as you thought," said Pangloss. "A medical school bought my body for dissection and a surgeon took me to his mortuary. He made an incision from my breast to my navel.

"I had been shockingly badly hanged. The High Executioner was excellent at having people shot, but as for hanging, he was not used to it. The rope was wet and did not slip properly, and the noose was too tight. In short, I continued to breath. The incision of the surgeon brought me back to consciousness and I roared out loud. The terrified man ran away as quickly as he could.

"I slowly recovered from my wounds but could not afford the proper care my injuries demanded. I eventually found employment as the tutor to the son of an ambassador, in which position I came to Istanbul.

"One day the boy who was my responsibility was discovered with a pretty young female when he should have been studying. I was instantly dismissed and found myself on these same streets as Penelope's brother. There are any number of homeless in this, as in most big cities and I have learnt that adventures similar to mine are very common.

"We have often argued as to whose is the worst misfortune. We were just disputing the point again when you appeared in front of us."

"Tell me, my dear Pangloss, when you had been hanged, cut open, dismissed, homeless and starving, did you still think that this was the perfect society?"

"I retain my first opinion. After all, I am an economist, and it would not become me to change my view. Besides, my misfortunes are my own, and my desire to overcome them, and the desire of others to avoid a similar fate, is what drives us."

Chapter Twenty-Nine

PENELOPE FOUND AGAIN

As the party approached the restaurant, they saw Penelope and the old woman cleaning the tables outside.

Penelope's brother turned pale at the sight, and even Candide, that faithful lover, was horrified. The lovely Penelope's skin was wrinkled and weather-beaten, her eyes were bloodshot, her neck withered and her arms and legs covered in red blotches. Candide recoiled for an instant, but good manners made him go forward. Penelope and the old woman embraced Candide and the brother. Candide paid the restaurant owner a small amount and they were free to leave.

The old woman suggested that Candide should rent a small farmhouse outside the city as a temporary lodging for the whole party. Penelope did not realise that she had grown ugly, and nobody mentioned it to her. She reminded Candide of his promises in so forthright a manner that the good-natured youth did not dare to refuse her. He told the brother that he was going to marry his sister.

"I will never allow such baseness on my sister's part," he replied, "or such insolence on yours. I will never allow myself to be reproached with such a disgrace. Why, my sister's children would not be welcome in any of the fine houses of England! No, my sister shall never marry any person who is not her equal in society."

Penelope fell weeping at her brother's feet.

"Silly fellow," said Candide, "have I not just delivered you from destitution, and rescued Penelope, too, who was a dish-washer and is very ugly? I have the goodness to make her my wife and you seek to oppose it? If I were to give rein to my anger, I would kill you again."

"I care not," said the obstinate brother. "I will never agree to this marriage while I am living."

Chapter Thirty

PHILOSOPHY ON THE BOSPHORUS

At the bottom of his heart, Candide had no wish to marry Penelope. But the brother's insolence made him determined to do so, and Penelope pressed him so warmly that he could not recant.

He consulted Pangloss, Martin and Cacambo. Pangloss drew up a fine memorandum setting out in detail why the lady was free to choose her own match, despite the wishes of her family. Martin advised throwing the brother into the sea. Cacambo suggested that he be drugged and abandoned on the streets near to where they had found him.

This suggestion received general favour. The old woman was told of it, and approved, but nothing was said about it to Penelope. The operation was carried out, to the satisfaction of all involved.

The reader might well suppose that Candide – having after so many misadventures, got married to his mistress; being blessed with the company of the economist Pangloss and the contrarian Martin, the shrewd Cacambo and the old woman; and having, moreover, brought back so many diamonds from the land of the ancient Incas – would now live happily ever after.

What in fact happened was this: Candide was cheated so badly by the diamond merchants that in the end he had nothing but his little farmhouse. His wife, who grew uglier every day, became bad-tempered and insupportable. The old woman was ailing, and became even worse-humoured than Penelope. Cacambo, who worked in the garden, became worn out with toil and felt utterly miserable. Pangloss was gloomy at not being a 'shining light' at some leading English university. As for Martin, he was convinced that one is equally badly off, wherever one is, so he bore everything with patience.

Candide, Martin and Pangloss sometimes had discussions on sociology, ethics and economics. Every day the papers brought stories of disasters, wars, famines and bankruptcies. Such news increased the philosophers' zeal for argument.

When they were not arguing, time hung so heavily on their hands that one day the old woman remarked: I wonder which is worse: to be ravished a hundred times by Zampatu rebels, to catch the plague, to be hanged and dissected, to be a tramp, or to stay here doing nothing."

"That," said Candide, "is a very profound question." It started them off on further discussions. "I should like to know," she continued, "is it better to live a life of complete security, protected by society from all poverty, illness or disadvantage but unable to become rich, or to run the gauntlet between rags and riches, able to fail but also able to succeed?"

Martin's view was that some people would be happier under one system and some under the other, so it was best to try to have a mix of the two. Pangloss believed that there were sufficient numbers who would prefer the latter to make it worth sacrificing the others. Candide did not entirely agree, but could not make up his mind.

Something happened that confirmed Martin's view, made Candide hesitate even more, and even caused Pangloss some embarrassment. This was the arrival of Paquette and her banker. They were penniless, Paquette having quickly spent the money Candide had given her, and the banker having lost his job. They had parted, been reconciled, and had quarrelled again. The banker had been briefly imprisoned for fraud. Paquette continued to ply her trade wherever she went, but earned little by it.

"I told you," Martin said to Candide, "that your gift would soon be squandered, and would only make her miserable. You and Cacambo have worked your way through millions of dollars, yet you are no happier than the banker or Paquette."

Pangloss had a few observations to make to Paquette. "So, my poor child," he said. "You have been brought back to us again. Do you know that you cost me an arm and a leg? Ah me, to what you have been reduced – and what a world this is!"

This new arrival made them all philosophise more than ever.

There lived in the neighbourhood a famous hermit, who was generally considered the best philosopher in Turkey. One day they went to consult him. Pangloss, as their spokesman, said to the hermit: "Master, we come to entreat you to tell us, what is the best political and economic system for man to live under?"

"Why do you bother with such matters?" said the hermit. "Is it any concern of yours?"

"But sir," said Candide, "surely there is great evil and misfortune in the world and the impulse of man is to organise to improve his lot."

"Do you think it makes any difference?"

"What, then, should one do?"

"Mind your own business."

"I have been looking forward," said Candide, "to discussing with you the nature of political and economic power, the optimal allocation of resources, and the instruments of social control within a free society."

At these words the hermit shut the door in their faces.

The same day news had come of the assassination of the Prime Minister, and the death of a number of his bodyguards. This catastrophe had caused a considerable stir for a few hours. On their return from the hermit's house, the philosophers met a worthy old man taking the air at his door, under the shade of some orange trees. Pangloss, who besides being an economist was also keenly interested in gossip, asked him if he knew any further details.

"No," said the old man, "I have never in my life taken any interest in the affairs of presidents or of prime ministers, nor do I know who they are. I take the view that all those who meddle in politics tend to come to a miserable end, and deserve to do so. But I never enquire into the goings on in the city. I am content with sending thither for sale the fruits of my garden."

He invited the foreigners into his house, where his two daughters and two sons brought them home-made pastries and juices of various kinds, sugared oranges, pineapples, plums, dates and pistachio nuts.

"You must have a large estate," Candide said to the old man.

"I have no more than ten acres, which I dig with the help of my children. Labour holds off three great evils: tedium, vice and poverty."

On their way home, Candide thought over the old man's words. "This old worthy," said he, "seems to have created for himself a life more preferable to those of the six presidents with whom we dined."

"Rich men are often brought low again," said Pangloss, "and the poor lifted up. You know the story of the penniless entrepreneur, whose invention and hard work makes a fortune and creates work for thousands? You know also…"

"I know also," said Candide, "that we must attend to our garden."

"You are right," said Pangloss, "let us by our own labour contribute to the wider picture. Man was not born to be idle."

"Let us work, then, and not argue," said Martin. "It is the only way to render life supportable."

All the members of the little society entered into this laudable design, and set themselves to exercise their various talents. Penelope continued to be very ugly, but she became an excellent cook. Paquette embroidered. The old woman laundered. Even the banker turned out to be useful: he proved to be a very good carpenter, and even quite a decent fellow.

Pangloss would often say to Candide: "You see how everything turns out for the best? If you had not been kicked out of Sir Charles' mansion for the love of Mistress Penelope, had you not been arrested and flogged, had you not travelled all over South America by foot, had you not killed Penelope's brother, had you not lost your mules from El Dorado – why, you would not now be here, eating sugared fruits and pistachio nuts."

"That is excellently observed," said Candide. "But let us go and dig in the garden."